CAN'T ESCAPE

Mohammed Maxwel Hasan

This is a work of fiction. Names, characters, businesses, places, events and incidents are either the products of the author's imagination or used in a fictitious manner. Any resemblance to actual persons, living or dead, or actual events is purely coincidental.

© 2017 Mohammed Maxwel Hasan

Edited by Inspiredwriter Editing Services

All rights reserved.

ISBN-13: 978-1-7750538-0-4

Dedication

To my sister Amanda, whose never-ending encouragement propelled the completion of this story.

To the marketing support, thank you for spreading the word about this story. You know who you are.

And for you, dear reader. Thank you for being on this journey.

1

"You're up, Oliver."

Mrs. Wilkins encouraged her final year art students to share personal items in front of the class. Despite her colleagues' disapproval of hosting the "childish" Show and Tell in high school, Mrs. Wilkins organized it during the first week of school.

She gently gestured for Oliver Masque to rise from his seat. Her emerald green eyes tried locking onto Oliver's hazel pupils, but he refused to raise his head.

"Oliver, the class is waiting for you," Mrs. Wilkins chirped.

Oliver stayed put. He wasn't going to embarrass himself. Not again.

Mrs. Wilkins nervously tapped her fingernails on her mahogany wood desk. She glanced at the school clock. 9:00 a.m.

"You don't want to get a zero on this assignment, right?"

His classmates were glued to their phones, desperate that things will move along. Some of them muttered Oliver's reluctance being a waste of time.

"Forget about it, Miss! Olive has a pea-brain!"

Rick Chaser, the self-proclaimed class clown took delight in cutting through the tension. Monopolizing air time, Rick *always* wanted others to know his point of view.

Just as Mrs. Wilkins opened her mouth, Oliver steadily stood up. All eyes were fixated on him as he carefully stomped through the class. He took long, lethargic strides as he felt the judging orbs pierce through him with every step.

After what seemed to be an eternity, he positioned himself in front of the blackboard.

Mrs. Wilkins cleared her throat. "This is a safe space for everyone. We all make mistakes, but it doesn't mean we should laugh at others." Her voice trembled a bit, but maintained a tone of authority.

"Only if you're a doofus, then we have to laugh!" Rick bellowed. A wave of snickers filled the room while he folded his massive arms behind his head, smiling proudly at his response.

Mrs. Wilkins rapidly turned her head with her burning, emerald glare. "No. We don't. I'm sorry, Oliver. You can go ahead now," she said, crossing her legs.

Twenty-four pairs of judgmental eyes stared coldly at Oliver's meek appearance. He felt the force of their merciless gaze and clenched his left hand.

His sandpaper-like voice travelled across the room, "My name is Oliver and this is what I brought for today."

Girls giggled and typed on their smartphones while Rick laughed obnoxiously. Oliver tried to ignore the excruciating disengagement of the class.

He gracefully pulled out a shiny, vintage object from his jacket pocket. "This is a pen, and it actually belonged to my father. He wrote poetry for a living and bought this exotic item at a fancy auction. It's the last surviving one of its kind."

Mrs. Wilkins beamed. "Wow, that's amazing!"

Oliver began to curl up a crooked smile. "It's made from a rare sterling silver, and was handcrafted exclusively for the 14th century English royal families. My father used to say that this pen was fit for a king or queen."

The class drowned out Oliver with fervent murmurs about the upcoming concerts, sports games and banquets. A drip of sweat plunged from his forehead. He quickly wiped it away with his left palm.

"My father also used this pen for calligraphy. Some of his finest works took many hours, as he tried to perfect the strokes of Edwardian Script..."

A devious sneer crawled on Rick's face as he curved and angled the rubber band around his right pinkie. He drew it towards his palm, looped the projectile around his strong thumb, and firmly positioned it in at the peak of his forefinger. Rick was ready to lock and load.

"Uhh...this pen is also..." Oliver trembled.

Rick glanced towards the student on his left as he mouthed the words, "watch this." The tension in the rubber band tightened as he was prepared for launch.

Oliver tried to shake it off. "The pen has a lot of..."

SNAP!

The rubber band flew with lightning speed and landed between Oliver's eyes. He doubled back, surprised by the unexpected trajectory and accuracy from the third row of the class.

A student held his phone up for recording and yelled, "Do it, again!" People were high fiving one another and slapping the desks in delight.

Mrs. Wilkins stood up, stared at the class and spoke with a fierce tone. "Who did that?!"

The room quieted down to mere chuckles, but there was no

response.

Mrs. Wilkins grew increasingly frustrated. "Who. Did. That."

Silence. People crudely stared down at their laps, chilled to meet her emerald glare.

"Whoever did that must have incredible aim!" Rick boasted.

"Alright, that's it! Straight to the principal's office."

"Oh no! What did I do?" Rick mocked. His eyelids narrowed as he scoffed.

"Leave." Her velvet green bracelet jingled as she sternly pointed her right index finger towards the exit.

"This is so dumb." Rick muttered as he sprung from his chair and forcefully put it back behind him.

The rest of the class had horrid looks on their faces, but Oliver secretly wished he could do a cartwheel. Seeing Rick in a pitiful state made Oliver feel like he was on top of the world.

Oliver clasped his hands together with great delight. "Thanks, Mom."

2

Oliver's pupils dilated and a lukewarm, putrid feeling climbed up his throat. The room was spinning and he began losing the sharpness of vision. *Did I just make the same mistake again?*

Rick halted at the door and smugly turned around with lit up eyes like the lamps of a lighthouse.

"What did you say? Poor Olive boy called Mrs. Wilkins mommy!" Rick jeered. Everyone started to laugh.

"I-I'm sorry, so sorr-" Oliver stumbled.

"It's okay, Oliver. It's fine. Class, class!" Mrs. Wilkins tried to command order amidst chaos, but it was too late.

Regaining his senses, Oliver shoved Rick out of the way, bolted past the class door, and ran furiously in the hallway. Roaring laughter kept replaying in his head as he slammed the bathroom door and ran the water through the sink. He washed his face excessively, avoiding his painful reflection in the stained mirror.

Oliver bitterly retrieved his pen. The object that was supposed to bring him a sense of pride ended up being connected to humiliation. He grazed his fingers over the intricate design, turned it over in his left palm and clenched it tightly. He was milliseconds away from crushing it to bits. Instead, he put it back in the inside of his jacket and wrapped himself in a bear hug.

I can't stay here.

Oliver stormed out of the gutted bathroom and navigated towards the school stairwell. His thunderous footsteps echoed as he flew down the marble stairs from the third floor to the first. He pushed open the door and ended up at the main entrance.

They don't care about me. Even if I'm gone.

Oliver briskly passed a group of students, who sat on a maroon bench chatting nonstop. Oliver ignored their rowdy conversation and marched ahead towards the nearby traffic lights.

The dingy traffic light turned fire red. Oliver waited impatiently at the curb for the crimson hand symbol to turn into a green pedestrian. A pudgy crossing guard flashed Oliver a smile.

"Nice day, isn't it?" the crossing guard said, making a sweeping gesture with her right arm.

No reply. The crossing guard tipped her head towards the sky. "You know, I love this area a lot. We get to see all kinds of seasons. Even if we get harsh weather, it won't last."

The traffic light turned from fiery red to cool green. The pedestrian symbol lit up instantly.

"You have yourself a good one, kiddo." The crossing guard waddled ahead of him, and when she got to the middle of the road, she stopped and outstretched her arms with a giant stop sign.

Oliver ignored her and jogged towards the sidewalk on the opposite side. The full-size, jet black sign loomed into view: "Altitude Apartments: Where you belong." There were four towering apartments, resembling giants among the landscape.

Almost there.

He steadily jogged until he reached his apartment's

entrance. Rows of last names and intercom entry buzz codes were plastered on the left wall encased with glass.

He dug deep in his pockets and pulled out a shiny, silver key. He rapidly inserted it in the keyhole, rotated it to the right and heard the sharp click. Oliver swung the door open and rushed towards the elevator lobby.

"You know, I can't believe she did that. I specifically told her not to put pickles in my sandwich and what does she do? The *exact* opposite." A lady in a cherry red cap ranted loudly.

"Must be the end of the world," her friend replied, adjusting her sky blue beanie.

"I know! I mean, how hard is it to get a simple order right?" the cherry cap lady proclaimed.

DING!

Oliver and the ladies piled into the elevator. The sky blue beanie pressed "4" while Oliver pressed "10."

"Seriously, though. I didn't enjoy my sandwich at all. I mean, you can take the pickles out, but you know it's already touching the rest of the sandwich and it's just ughh!"

DING!

The two ladies stepped off the fourth floor, and the rambling subsided as the tanned doors slowly closed together.

Oliver let out a huge sigh of relief. He stared blankly at the ceiling as the soft, whirring sound of the elevator steadily making its way up the floors contaminated the silence.

DING!

Oliver entered the tenth floor and strolled towards his apartment door on the right hallway. He fumbled for his keys and with an aggressive huff, unlocked the door and shut it behind him.

He stormed into his cramped bedroom, plopped into his prison corner and tightly wrapped his twig arms over his crouched legs. Oliver's shoulders trembled as he quietly wept with convulsive gasping.

3

Oliver groggily dragged his sagging gaze at the bedroom clock. 4:39 a.m.

He sluggishly rubbed his eyes as he unravelled himself from the crouched position. He blinked back tears as he slowly got up.

His bulky laptop was the only centre piece of a crusty, wooden desk. The framed envelope labelled "Oliver Masque" was placed discretely on the top left corner.

Oliver flipped open the laptop and a bright, neon "Welcome" message appeared. He involuntarily squinted as if he was staring at the blazing flares of the sun. Immediately, Oliver grabbed his mouse and clicked on the Surfer icon, his preferred web browser.

He hurriedly typed in the search engine and stopped halfway as the browser recognized his most frequently visited site: Two Cents. It was a social media platform where people shared their lives. People either chose to be anonymous or identifiable. Oliver decided to be anonymous, yet he saved a list of classmates who publicly announced their updates.

On the homepage, there were active threads well underway. The most popular one of the day was titled "Baby Olive."

RelishingRick: *Did u guys see Olive call Wilkins mommy? What a loser!*
Ace245: *Yeah, I was like totally shocked. Looks like someone needs therapy.*
Dennis2Dentist: *Oliver the Holler.*

Oliver angrily grinded his teeth as the insults kept going. *Lowlife. Crybaby. Failed abortion.*

Oliver slammed the laptop on the ground as his heart was furiously pumping out of his chest. With an animalistic desire to express his rage, Oliver began punching his old mattress over and over again. *It's not fair, it's not fair!!* With every hit he landed, the springs recoiled and emitted a squeaky sound. He punched until he was physically tired and drained.

Oliver didn't want to look back at the messages, but he hoped that he misread them. Maybe they were talking about a different Oliver.

He carefully picked up the laptop from the floor, checking to make sure nothing was broken. After examining the large scratch on the front, he placed it back on the centre of the table.

Oliver flipped open the laptop once again, and plucked his eyelashes as he scrolled down the page. The same insults hurled back at him. *Annoying. Loner. Waste of oxygen.*

Before Oliver shut everything down with misty-eyes, he caught another message. It was buried between the insults, but it was like a ray of sunshine within darkness.

Why don't you all cut it out? You're all being very rude and disrespectful. What if Oliver actually reads this? You all ought to be ashamed of yourselves.

Oliver re-read that post three times. He let the words sink in and quickly checked to see who wrote it. With a disappointed sigh, he found that the person was anonymous.

He desperately clicked on the profile to see if there were any clues for identification. Nothing. The profile avatar was a picture of two pennies in a square, the default setting for anonymous profiles.

Knock. Knock. Knock.

"Oliver? Are you there?"

Oliver quickly closed the laptop cover and sprinted towards the front door of his apartment. He peered through the peephole and noticed a white security outfit. Unlocking the door from the left side, he swung it open.

"What's going on, Deputy Jerry?"

Jerry was the apartment's main security guard, but insisted on being referred to as "Deputy." He was built like an ox, and a few inches taller than Oliver. He astutely looked down with penetrating ocean blue pupils.

"Someone on your floor made a phone call, saying that there was noise coming from your room. Like a loud crashing sound. Is everything alright?" Deputy Jerry asked.

"Yeah, everything is fine. I just dropped my laptop, that's all," Oliver replied.

"Okay, because safety is-"

"The number one priority. I know, Deputy."

Deputy Jerry rested his hand on Oliver's shoulder. "That's right. Remember, if you need anything, you can always talk to me."

Oliver patted Deputy Jerry's hand. "I know. Thanks."

"Now is probably not a good time, since you've got those bags under your eyes. But if you want to talk, you know where to find me." Deputy Jerry smiled.

"Right." Oliver tried to return the smile.

"Have a good night, or should I say a good dawn," Deputy Jerry tapped on his expensive, hefty watch.

"You too, Deputy." Oliver slowly shut the door with the

lock clicking into place. He strutted back to his room, glanced at the framed envelope and picked it up. He held it in his hands as his name stared back at him.

Deputy Jerry is a nice guy.

Oliver put the frame back in its place and exhaustingly crawled into bed. His heavy eyelids snapped shut against the dim light of dawn as he snored rhythmically.

4

The frying pan sizzled as the vegetable oil loudly popped. The chimney range hood whirred incessantly as Oliver's nose scrunched up while shaking the frying pan.

Once he determined the eggs were a golden brown, he placed them flatly on a dish and sat down on the small kitchenette table. He grabbed a silverware fork and knife from the drawer and primly cut the eggs.

Juice. He needed juice. Oliver leapt to his feet and scoured his fridge. The remaining eggs in the carton, some leftover fries and packets of noodles were haphazardly placed like a twister through a trailer park.

The filling life of a student.

He reached towards the bottom right corner and pulled out a half-filled carton of orange juice. It made a swishing sound as he poured himself a tall glass.

As Oliver munched on his eggs, he thought about Deputy Jerry's offer. Maybe he did need someone to talk with about the disastrous presentation. After all, Oliver respected him and noticed his superb communication skills, even when people gave him a hard time.

Oliver chuckled as he recalled an incident involving a baffled, elderly man with his internet security access. Even though Deputy Jerry suggested talking to an IT expert, he kept insisting it was security's fault for having slow Wi-Fi and not being able to connect to "The Promised LAN" network.

Oliver slurped the rest of his orange juice and began walking out the door. He locked it behind him and took three steps away. Oliver twisted his head and frantically went back to check to see if it was still locked. He jiggled the door knob until he was satisfied that it was secure.

The thought of talking to Deputy Jerry filled him with a burst of energy and he raced down ten flights of stairs.

Panting, Oliver trotted towards the far end of the elevator lobby. He gazed up at the navy blue "Security" sign on top of the mini, milky white kiosk, which could fit only one or two people at a time.

"Hello," a gruff security guard greeted through the glass.

"Is Deputy Jerry here?"

"He's about to leave for lunch. Better luck next time."

Oliver pouted. His lower lip quivered a little as he sunk his head.

In a moment's notice, Deputy Jerry appeared from behind the kiosk. "Hi Oliver! Just caught me in time. Want to join me for lunch?"

Oliver's stomach growled out of excitement. "Sure."

"See you later, Wayne!" Deputy Jerry waved to the plump security guard seated at the kiosk.

They left the apartment and strolled across the ground level parking lot. Deputy Jerry led the way to his vintage, sapphire convertible and manually unlocked the doors with the key.

"How does the Honey Garden sound?" Deputy Jerry asked, as he eased himself in the grainy leather driver's seat.

"Great."

The engine revved and Deputy Jerry reached over to turn on Vortex News.

"That's great Diane. I think the Write Speech competition is going be phenomenal this year. There's always something to hear from these wonderful speakers."

"Well, what do you know? That competition sounds exciting," Deputy Jerry remarked.

Yeah, right. Oliver rolled back his eyes. The news continued to natter away for the remainder of the short ride.

They arrived at the restaurant and parked near the front entrance. The two trekked to an empty table and opened the bountiful menu.

"I'm going for the Honey Special. What about you?" Deputy Jerry set down his menu.

Oliver stared at the food options. He couldn't decide which one to pick, as they were all out of his price range. Even the silky, jade tablecloth gave the impression of prestige.

"I invited you to lunch, so it's on me. What does your heart tell you to order?" Deputy Jerry smiled.

Oliver hesitated and just as he was about to answer, a young waitress emerged.

"Welcome to The Honey Garden. May I take your orders?" the waitress beamed.

"One Honey Special for me," Deputy Jerry said. The bubbly waitress jotted it down and immediately glanced at Oliver.

"Me too," Oliver said.

"Wonderful. I'll be sure to bring them as soon as they're done." She disappeared to serve the other tables.

Deputy Jerry's penetrating gaze probed Oliver. "So, what's on your mind?"

Oliver dumped all his feelings onto Deputy Jerry. He told him about the embarrassing Show and Tell pen presentation to the hurtful online comments.

"-and I saw one nice person try to stand up for me. But I don't know who did it." Oliver's head sunk and quietly sniffled.

Deputy Jerry rubbed his strong chin and spoke. "What your classmates was inexcusable. But guess what? I think I know what you need to do."

"What?"

"You need to become a professional public speaker."

Oliver quickly rose his head up with one eye twitching. "What?"

Didn't he just hear what I went through? Was I wrong telling him all this?

"Now, now, hear me out. Even though you had a bad presentation, it doesn't mean you're bad. If you truly want to have people respect you, you have to learn how to express yourself in a dignified and professional manner. Take it from me. Believe it or not, you don't always run into nice people as a security guard. But I have to know how to conduct myself if I want to maintain my sanity."

Oliver stared coldly and strongly shook his head until it almost fell off his shoulders.

"Call it fate or what-have-you, but you remember the news radio talking about a speakers competition? I was planning on participating, but because of my work schedule, there's been a change in plans. If you gave it a try, it could be like me mentoring you. Here."

> WANT TO BE INFLUENTIAL, BOLD, AND BE AMONG THE STARS IN
> THE PUBLIC SPEAKING INDUSTRY?
> TAKE PART IN THE WRITE SPEECH NATIONAL COMPETITION!
>
> DUE TO THE HIGH VOLUME OF SUBMISSIONS, WRITE **1 SENTENCE**
> AS TO WHY YOU SHOULD BE IN THIS COMPETITION
>
> THE WINNERS OF THE FIRST ROUND WILL BE ANNOUNCED
> PUBLICLY ON MONDAY

Oliver swiftly scanned through the advert. The call for submissions will end in two days.

"Think about it, Oliver. Oh look, our orders are here."

Deputy Jerry happily chomped on the Honey Garden special. The tangy aroma of honey dressing, mixed in with spiced pecans and topped with savoury parmesan pasta filled their nostrils.

Oliver gave a final momentary glance, creased the advertisement into his pocket, and devoured his meal.

5

Oliver gripped the wrinkled paper and kept replaying his lunchtime memory with Deputy Jerry in his head. It was midnight and Oliver sat solemnly hunched over at his bedroom desk.

Oliver rubbed the sides of his temples and ran his coarse, bony fingers over his thick, wavy hair.

Should I do this? People will just laugh at me again. Besides, who am I? I'm just a nobody. Everyone thinks I'm a joke. Me, Oliver Masque, a public speaker? Stop kidding yourself and leave this alone.

Oliver stepped away from his desk, and held his hands to his hips. He paced back and forth in front of his bed, hammering himself.

This is so stupid. Deputy Jerry doesn't actually believe I have a chance. He was just talking to be nice. Nobody cares about me.

The sound of crinkled paper cut through the silence of the room. In a swift motion, Oliver rolled up the handout into a ball and tightly clasped it into his left fist.

He wandered over to his kitchenette. Hovering above the trash bin, he promptly stepped on the pedal and stared down at disposed banana peels, traces of rice pudding, and rotten apple slices.

Oliver chucked the paper right in the middle of the food mess. He lifted his foot off the pedal and triumphantly dusted his hands off.

What a ridiculous idea. I almost fell for it.

Oliver went back to his bedroom, booted up his laptop and checked Two Cents. The most popular thread of the day featured, "How to be annoyingly likeable." Hundreds of strangers from around the globe participated in the discussion. Unconcerned, Oliver clicked away from the main menu and landed on the "Baby Olive" thread. No new responses.

Just as Oliver was about to click away from the page, he glanced at the anonymous message again.

Why don't you all cut it out? You're all being very rude and disrespectful. What if Oliver actually reads this? You all ought to be ashamed of yourselves.

Oliver blinked once, twice.

Maybe someone does care about me.

His hazel gaze darted over at the exquisite pen, anchored on the side of the desk. He picked it up and caressed it with both hands as the silver grazed his fingertips.

Oliver turned towards the framed note sitting on the desk corner. He placed the pen down gently and grabbed the frame with a trembled right hand.

If I don't tell my story, who will?

Oliver calmly set down the frame. He sat up, scurried over to the kitchenette and leaned over the trash can. He forcefully stomped on the pedal and the lid flipped open with all the disposed gunk. He wearily reached in and snatched the crumpled advertisement.

Ugh.

Pieces of rice pudding clung on to the side of the paper. Oliver flicked off the pieces and retreated to the bedroom. He unfolded the advertisement and smoothed it out on the desk.

He turned it over, took hold of his pen and with delicate writing etched "Attempt 1" across the top of the page.

What should I write about myself? He decided to write down the first thing that came to his head.

"I think I have a story to tell."

No, too general and doesn't actually say anything. He crossed it out and underneath wrote "Attempt 2."

"If you like amazing things, you'll love my speech."

Better, but still doesn't say much.

Oliver kept trying, listing attempt after attempt.

"Check out this underdog."

"From zero to hero."

"Not just talking the talk, but walking the walk."

Nothing felt right to Oliver. Soon, the single sheet filled up and his hand started to feel inflamed at the wrist joint.

I'm missing something. Maybe I need a new angle or perspective.

Oliver got up, arched his back and felt a relieving spinal crack. He waddled to the bathroom sink and splashed cold water on his tired face. He scowled at his pitiful reflection.

If only my reflection could show me what's inside.

Oliver rubbed more water on his face and then dried himself with a towel.

Wait, that's it!

Oliver quickly put the towel on the towel rack and ran back to the bedroom. He scribbled down his sentence in a hurry and excitedly started up the laptop.

He visited the Write Speech website and followed the instructions for initial submissions. Oliver gleefully grinned as he looked back at the erratic handwriting and typed out every word. He constantly checked and rechecked to make sure every letter matched.

Hope this works.

Oliver clicked "Send" and a confirmation message flashed before him. Without turning off the laptop, he climbed into bed.

***

A deep ditch spanned a few metres wide. Oliver stood on one end above the ditch, while a golden microphone floated on the opposing end. A multitude of red roses dwelled at the bottom of the ditch.

Oliver gawked at the golden microphone and desperately desired it. He took a few steps backwards, sped up, leaped valiantly, but he miscalculated the jump.

Oliver fell down the ditch and landed nimbly on the bed of roses. He panicked, and suddenly the roses mutated into dark, spiky microphones. Inch by inch, they started engulfing him and Oliver cried out with a howling scream.

Oliver woke up in a cold sweat, testing his pulse and examining his skin to make sure there were no prick marks. After a few deep breaths, he rested his head on the plush pillow and slowly drifted off back to sleep.

6

BRRING!
Mrs. Wilkins' students shuffled around to their seats while chatting about their weekends. Talks about the latest movies, parties attended and how much they overslept filled the air.

Oliver quietly sat by himself at the back. He listened carefully to the fascinating conversations that took place. He was initially hesitant to come to class, thinking people would bring up the horrific "Mom" incident. But, nobody looked in his direction or even bothered to ask about his weekend.

"Whoo! Those tape selfies were hi-lar-i-ous!"

Rick barged in and hi-fived a few peers. He whipped out his phone and started scrolling through a myriad of photos.

"Yo, we taped our faces and put them online. You should see this guy's face. He looks like a deranged pig!" Rick laughed.

Mrs. Wilkins stepped through the doorway, carrying a stack of ruffled papers. She set down the heavy load on her desk like a pile of bricks.

"Good morning, class. Sorry I'm a bit late; traffic was pretty bad on the way over here. Before we get into today's lesson on Cubism art, there's some interesting news here." Mrs. Wilkins smiled.

She yanked out the local newspaper amidst the batch of paperwork and smoothed out the crinkles. "Write Speech Competitor Advancement" was boldly marked on the front page. Oliver perked up.

"The Write Speech convention is the largest public speaking

competition. It features renowned speakers from all over the globe. People of eloquence and mastery of stage presence participate." Mrs. Wilkins read out the description and pointed to the picture of the competition's logo.

Students began losing interest and yawned profusely.

"Don't worry, it gets better. Today, they just released the names of the top 20 submissions." Mrs. Wilkins adjusted her glasses as she turned the paper towards her.

"Let's see: there's Susan Krist, Cameron Hewitson, Erin Cruz...and well, well, well, look who we have here." Mrs. Wilkins smiled even more.

For a few seconds, the class stopped staring at their phones and turned their attention Mrs. Wilkins.

"Rick Chaser is in the top 20."

Rick raised his large fist in the air and howled loudly. "I'm the MAN!"

"Wow, I didn't know you were into public speaking." Mrs. Wilkins remarked.

"Are you kidding me? I *love* talking. I guess they loved my sentence: 'The mass with class will reach through speech.' " Rick propped up his feet and clasped his arms behind the back of his head.

Oliver solemnly sunk his head.

"Congratulations, Rick. Although you have a special talent of getting under people's skin, all the best on the competition. But wait, there's another speaker in the top 20 in this room." Mrs. Wilkins beamed.

She pointed her finger towards the back of the class. "Oliver Masque."

The class gasped and turned around simultaneously. Rick almost fell out of his chair. Oliver jolted up and blinked owlishly around as they inspected him with pure disgust. He heard pieces of whispers.

"That momma's boy made it?"

"Oliver wants to talk?"

Oliver steadily sunk in his seat. *I actually advanced to the auditions?*

"Well, it looks like we've got some amazing potential in this class. Good luck, Oliver and Rick." Mrs. Wilkins said.

Rick carefully stroked his jaw and severely glared at Oliver. He tried to ignore it, but felt Rick's gaze suffocating and stifling.

"Please open your textbooks to page 134. We're discussing how art and architecture fused..."

He didn't pay attention to a single word. Oliver was still absorbing the news. *Imagine me getting first place. Rick will be devastated and everyone else will finally respect me.*

He daydreamed about graciously receiving the first place prize while Rick cried in a corner. Oliver's lips drew up a coy smile at that thought.

BRRING!

"Wow, that went fast. Remember to write a one page reflection on the article we just read." Mrs. Wilkins hollered over the noise of students packing up their bags.

Oliver snapped out of a daze, jammed his belongings and headed towards the door.

"Hey, Olive. Mind if I speak to you for a second?" Rick called out.

Oliver was spellbound.

"Uhh...sure."

They stepped outside the classroom and stood in front of the smoky lockers. Oliver adjusted the straps of his backpack as Rick keenly leaned in towards him.

"Congratulations on being in the top 20." Rick extended his burly right hand.

Oliver gripped his strap as he nervously glanced down at Rick's hand. Rick's shadowy eyes fluttered.

Is this some sort of prank? Maybe he's trying to be nice.

"Well, thanks."Oliver loosened his grip on the strap and reached out to Rick's hand. Rick seized it tightly and forcibly brought his arm closer to him.

"If you think for a second that you are going to beat me, think again. You are nothing but a low-life, wannabe reject. No one has ever liked you, no one likes you and no one will ever like you. You understand? So, save yourself the embarrassment and drop out of this competition. You'll be doing everyone a favour."

Rick deviously sneered, slammed Oliver's arm against the lockers and strolled away.

Oliver grasped his throbbing hand, terror-stricken and disorientated.

7

"Is Deputy Jerry there?"

Oliver continuously fidgeted while talking to the plump security guard behind glass. His fingers nervously tapped on the cool, white counter.

"Let me check. Jerry!"

"Yeah?" a voice called back.

"Someone wants to see you."

Deputy Jerry appeared as his polished, shield-shaped badge glistened across his broad chest.

"Oliver! What can I do for you?" Deputy Jerry grinned.

"Can I talk to you in private?" Oliver said quietly.

Deputy Jerry sensed the quiver in his voice. "Sure thing. I will be with you in a minute."

Deputy Jerry disappeared in the back, leaving Oliver alone with the plump security guard. He grunted and started flipping through pages of his daily log form.

"I'm only useful when danger calls," he mumbled.

Oliver stayed silent. He wasn't sure if that was an invitation to inquire or just talking out loud. The rustling of paper and the exasperated exhaling made Oliver feel awkward.

Finally, Deputy Jerry stepped outside the kiosk and motioned Oliver to follow him. The two moved down the hallway, passed the elevators and into a small room. Deputy Jerry flipped open the light switch and gestured Oliver to have a seat.

The room was cramped and dull, featuring only two chairs and gray walls.

"This area is for private conversations and a place for me to say a few stern words here and there to some noisy apartment tenants. So, what's on your mind?"

"I got accepted for the Write Speech auditions."

"That's wonderful! See, I knew you had it in you." Deputy Jerry lightly punched Oliver's shoulder for moral support. "What's the problem?"

Oliver hesitated to speak.

"Come on. You can tell me." Deputy Jerry shifted closer.

"There's...this guy in my class, Rick. He's also in the auditions, but he threatened me to stay out of his way." Oliver tugged at his collar. "I was...pretty scared."

Deputy Jerry leaned back slowly, breathed out softly as he crossed his arms and stared down into the depths of Oliver's hazel eyes.

"You listen to me. Don't let Rick intimidate you. Sounds like *he's* the one threatened by you in the competition. Look, Oliver, people like that are filled with hot air. It's like the saying goes: 'you get what you tolerate.' "

Something about Deputy Jerry's words made Oliver feel giddy and immune to danger. Oliver earnestly shook his head up and down. "Ok."

Deputy Jerry mirrored Oliver's nod. "Believe me, you've got something special in you. And I want you to know that I'll always be here for you."

Oliver swelled up inside. Those words felt good. "Thanks, Deputy Jerry."

Deputy Jerry shifted gears and spoke in an enthusiastic voice. "Well, you're embarking on a new challenge in your life!

I'll do my best to help you achieve that goal of becoming a public speaker."

He scanned Oliver from top to bottom. "I hate to break it to you, kid, but we've got a lot of work to do. People are ruthless and some don't have an ounce of respect for hard work. It's like that saying goes: 'you don't get a second chance at a first impression.' "

Oliver felt like this was going to be his superhero origin story. He smirked at his own foolish thought of being in a cape flying around, with a super powered microphone blasting away evil.

"The first step is to take care of your voice. Imagine you're about to deliver the world's most important message and your voice isn't clear. How do you think people will react?"

Oliver shrugged his shoulders. "I guess you're right."

"Oh! Luckily, there's this person I know who is a trained, voice specialist. The best part is that she lives right here in this apartment, room 500. I think you will find her exceptional. Her name is Dr. Hailey Bell."

Deputy Jerry rose from his seat. "Alright, Oliver, that's a good starting point for now. Go meet with her and tell her I sent you."

He started to exit the room before he stopped and shot Oliver a glowering look.

"By the way, what was the sentence you submitted to advance the next round?"

"I'll let you know later."

"Keeping surprises, are we? Well, when the time is right, let me know." He left the confined room.

Oliver stayed motionless. He had a dream, a mentor and a plan.

Goodbye, old me.

8

Dear Oliver,

Congratulations! You have been selected to advance to the next round of the Write Speech competition. As you know, we value the importance of writing clearly and succinctly. Now, this is the time to verbalize those eloquent words. Your task is to create a 20 second video of yourself speaking about what makes you unique. Once again, congratulations on advancing to the next round and happy filming!

-Write Speech

Oliver 's mind was hooked on the recent email he received as he pressed the cool, elevator button. The bright, yellow outline illuminated the button as he perpetually tapped his foot.

My pen? My DNA? My loneliness? What makes me unique?
DING!

Oliver hopped on and positioned himself at the left corner as the doors slid smoothly. He pressed "5" with his thumb and the elevator started to rise.

"Don't you just hate it when your contacts get stuck in your eye?"

Oliver averted his gaze and saw the familiar cherry red cap. *Oh no, not again.*

"I mean, it's just like..ugh! I try to blink and my eye keeps getting redder and redder. It's sooo unattractive and it hurts," the cherry cap lady said a mile a minute, using her right index finger to curl up her eyelids.

"Someone, call 911," her friend said sarcastically.

DING!

Oliver hurriedly got off the fifth floor. *Does that girl ever stop talking?*

He crept through the hallway and keenly tracked the decelerating numbers. *511. 510. 509.* Oliver proceeded until he reached the final unit on the right side of the hallway. *500.*

He stood in front of the door, admiring the "Voice 4 You" sign plastered across the top in funky letters. He planted his feet, took a deep breath and knocked three times. Silence. He knocked three more times, with a little more vigour.

Oliver pressed his ear up onto the door, waiting for a response. Immediately, he felt self-conscious at how suspicious he looked.

Finally, he heard some faint footsteps headed towards the door. A large peep hole slid out and the sound of chains jiggling made Oliver take a tiny step back.

Suddenly, the door swung open and a rather short lady appeared. She was dressed in a maroon bathrobe and tied her hair in a bun. "May I help you?"

Oliver gulped. "H-hi, are you Dr. Hailey Bell?"

"Yes." She glared at Oliver, examining him.

"Well..." Oliver coughed to clear up his hoarse voice. "Deputy Jerry recommended that I should talk to you for voice improvement?"

At once, Dr. Bell's crystal blue eyes twinkled. "Deputy Jerry sent you? Oh my! By all means, come on in!" She gestured Oliver to go inside and he obediently entered.

As she closed the door behind her, the aroma of frothy chocolate filled the air. "I'm just brewing some nice cocoa. Would you like some?"

"Sure, thanks." Oliver carefully took off his shoes and his white socks grazed the smooth carpet.

"Alright, you can make your way to the sofa right over there. I'll bring the cocoa," Dr. Bell said.

Oliver strolled through the living room to sit on the genuine leather sofa. It seemed relatively new and there was a slight squeak as his denim pants made contact with the leather. He marvelled at the mouth anatomy posters, graduate school certificates and letters of appreciation to Dr. Bell.

"So, how is Deputy Jerry? He's helped me out a lot, especially when those hoodlums next door are causing such a ruckus." Dr. Bell sat beside Oliver and set down the mugs of cocoa on the circular, glass table.

"He's doing well."

"Wonderful! What can I do for you?"

"I'm in the Write Speech competition and the submission for video auditions is next week. Deputy Jerry says my voice needs to be clearer. Can you help me?"

"Well, I won't be able to do a full treatment prognosis, but I can do a couple of simple tests with you right now. Open your mouth."

Oliver obediently stuck his tongue out. Dr. Bell pulled out a mini flashlight and aimed the beam at his tonsils. "It looks like your uvula is irritated, and there seems to be vocal damage."

She put away the flashlight. "Since you only have a week for this competition, a simple thing you can start doing right now is to drink ginger tea. It's a known flavour that will help make your voice seamless. I carry them around me all the time." She gave Oliver a ginger tea bag.

"And also, don't keep clearing your throat by forcibly doing it. It actually irritates the muscles."

Oliver couldn't contain his excitement. "Thank you, Dr. Bell. I don't want to take up any more of your time, so I guess I better get going now." Oliver stood up and almost knocked over the mugs.

"Oops, careful! Don't you want your cocoa?" Dr. Bell asked.

"It's okay, I need to get going now." Oliver replied, holding up the ginger tea bag.

"Suit yourself. Hope your competition goes well and say hi to Deputy Jerry for me," Dr. Bell flashed a smile.

Oliver put on his shoes, did a little wave and left Dr. Bell's apartment. Armed with ginger tea and a newfound sense of ambition, he was ready to start filming.

9

Pairs of socks, shirts and pants flew across the room as Oliver frantically rummaged through his closet to find his best clothes to wear. *Where is it?*

After a painstaking search, he finally found his white dress shirt. It was the only one he possessed, a backup in case if there was a remote chance he got invited to fancy events.

Oliver slipped on the white collared shirt and started buttoning the black casein buttons up. He wished he had a tie and blazer to match, but this was all he could afford. Oliver peered through the closet and pulled out his slim, charcoal dress pants from a hanger.

After assembling his outfit, Oliver shuffled to his living room. The washed-out wallpaper suited Oliver's taste for a backdrop. Although it wasn't extravagant, the simple background would draw focus on him.

On the living room table, he stacked his old textbooks from previous classes: physics, chemistry, and psychology. The thick textbooks wobbled like they were on a tightrope, but he managed to stabilize them.

Oliver situated his laptop on the highest book. He constantly made adjustments to make sure the built-in webcam caught a decent field of vision. The quality wasn't the greatest, not even close to the popular products his classmates had, but it was sufficient.

After a few tweaks, Oliver was satisfied with the positioning. He went to the kitchenette and carefully poured himself a mug of ginger tea. It was scorching hot as the steam swiftly rose to the ceiling. Oliver carried the mug with him to the living room and cautiously set it down on the table beside the leaning tower of books. As he waited for it to cool down, Oliver planned what he wanted to say.

"Good morni-no. Hi, I'm Oliver and this is my video submission for the contest."

Too boring.

"Oliver Masque here and let me tell you why I'm great."

Too arrogant.

"Oliver's the name and speaking is my game."

Too cheesy.

He went over dozens of potential introductions. Each one lacked a noteworthy moment. He constantly got up and paced around whenever he was stuck, or jotted notes on scrap paper. Sipping his ginger tea, Oliver thought profusely.

At last, he settled on his pitch. *Time to record.* Oliver sat down on the scuffed couch, adjusted his shirt slightly and swept bangs out of his face. In a delicate fashion, he pressed "Record" on his laptop, trying his best not to make it collapse.

Oliver instinctively spread out his fingers in the air as he slowly inched away from the laptop. With a sharp inhale, he began.

"Hi, I'm Oliver Masque and loneliness is my uniqueness. I may not have many friends, or get invited to many social gatherings, but I know what it's like to face this world alone."

Oliver recorded and re-recorded his video over the course of a week. Sometimes, he tripped over his own words or he didn't feel like the video captured the desired emotion. Oliver continuously drank the ginger tea and practiced voice exercises he discovered online. He knew he wasn't going to magically have a deep, captivating, baritone voice, but he noticed it was getting clearer.

He checked the various footage stored on his laptop. Oliver sorted through the files and located the best version.

Oliver incessantly clicked on the icon of Vedit, the video editing software automatically installed in his laptop.

Once the program loaded, Oliver clicked on "Import" and located his file. He dragged and dropped down the video clip to the working area. With a few clicks, Oliver added a title that would appear at the bottom of the clip and he trimmed it so that the awkward pauses in the beginning and at the end would be erased.

After adding a few finishing touches, Oliver saved the video onto his desktop in the highest quality possible. He apprehensively tapped his fingers on the table and kept muttering to himself as the file generated.

Eventually, the loading completed and Oliver reviewed it once more, to make sure there were no technical errors.

Without delay, Oliver started drafting an email, with smoke coming out of his lightning-fast fingers.

Hi Write Speech,

Thank you for the opportunity to advance. Attached with this email is my video submission. I hope you like it.

Sincerely,

Oliver

He gulped down the remaining ginger tea as the cursor hovered over "Send." With a deep breath, Oliver clicked and the message disappeared.

10

"We're going to be doing a mind mapping exercise about how art influences modern society. I'll break you all into teams of three, and just to make things a bit interesting, I'll number you off."

Mrs. Wilkins beamed excitedly at the prospect of students meeting each other, in spite of the moans and groans of protest. Her emerald bracelet rattled as she made the count.

"Okay, just remember your number. One, two, three. One, two, three..."

Oliver, sitting in the back, was mentally calculating his assigned number. He kept track of the people already selected and hoped to be a "One."

Mrs. Wilkins got closer to Oliver's area. Her magnetic look caught Oliver and said, "Three."

Great.

Mrs. Wilkins finished distributing the numbers. "One's go to the front of the class. Two's go to the middle and three's go to the back of the class."

Everyone staggered around to position themselves with their respective teams. Oliver discreetly pulled up a chair to sit with his fellow teammates, but they didn't glance up at his arrival. Some of their heads tilted backward, staring at the ceiling while others made popping sounds with their mouths.

As long as I don't bother anyone, they shouldn't bother me.

"You've got to be kidding me!" a loud voice bellowed.

Rick slapped his hand across his forehead and let out a huge groan. "I'm with Olive? Miss! Can we have a do-over?"

Mrs. Wilkins' glare traveled over towards Rick's direction. "No. You are with team three."

Rick let out an exasperated sigh. "But I don't want to. Can't I-"

"That's enough, Rick. You are on this team and that's final." Mrs. Wilkins' emerald pupils glared viciously.

Rick reluctantly sat down in the back of the room. "This is so stupid," he muttered.

Oliver tried to pretend Rick's behaviour didn't bother him as Mrs. Wilkins strolled around with large pieces of paper and coloured markers. Her stern gaze sliced Rick as she set down the materials.

"What you need to do is make a simple mind map of art and modern society. Afterwards, the teams will present their work to the class. Happy mind mapping!"

There was a solid thirty seconds of Team Three silence. Finally, Rick piped up and said, "Let's get his dumb assignment over with."

He reached over and grabbed the red marker and drew a big oval in the middle. He started writing "Art" in the middle and branched out to other circles.

"Whoa, whoa, what are you doing?" Oliver asked.

"None of your business, Olive." Rick retorted and continued drawing.

Oliver stayed silent. The rest of the teammates' beady pupils ogled curiously.

"One more minute and then we'll share!" Mrs. Wilkins exclaimed.

Rick sketched in a few more circles and filled them with

headings. "Ok, we're done."

Oliver thought it was ironic that Rick said "we," but decided not to say anything. The other teammates couldn't care less.

"Okay! Time's up. Team One, what did you come up with?" Mrs. Wilkins asked.

There were a few murmurs going back and forth about the designated presenter. Eventually, one of the girls stepped up.

"Hi, my name is Caroline. We came up with the theme of beauty." She scrunched up her freckled nose and pushed up her pink-rimmed glasses.

"Art comes in all shapes and sizes. It can be through paintings, literature or entertainment and other things. So, we collaborated and found examples like MC Esher's optical illusions or Edgar Allen Poe's poetry. Art conveys meaning and that meaning is up to you." Caroline sat down and folded her hands together.

"Impressive work, Team One! I'm really proud of how you all came up with that in such a short amount of time. Next up, Team Two," Mrs. Wilkins said.

A guy stood up. "Yeah, so we thought art was like abstract and stuff. So, yeah." He sat down.

Mrs. Wilkins blinked a few times. "Well, that's nice, James. Could you elaborate a bit further?"

James stood up again. "Actually, there's no right or wrong with art. It's what you make of it." He quickly sat down again.

"Okay, that's great! Wonderful job, Team Two! Last but not least, Team Three," Mrs. Wilkins smiled.

Oliver stared at Rick, expecting him to stand up without

any consultation. But to his surprise, Rick nudged Oliver. "Go ahead."

"No, I can't-"

"Just do it. Come on! You're in the Write Speech competition, aren't you?" Rick winked.

Oliver reluctantly stood up with the paper in hand. "Uhhh…well...you see..." Oliver drew a blank. He had no idea what Rick's intentions were when he wrote the information.

Some classmates shook their heads, while others had their faces crestfallen with embarrassment.

"Well, I guess I'll have to save the day." Rick stood up and snatched the paper from Oliver.

"You see, art is a powerful influence in society. When you see 'The Starry Night' painting, you think of innovation on a canvas. When you see 'The Persistence of Memory' painting, you think of the fragility of time. Art is everywhere you go."

The class was glued to Rick's performance. The way he swayed his arms while emphasizing each point hung people by the edge of their seats.

"From painting, to literature, art reminds us what it truly means to be human. The diverse interpretations reflect the diversity in human beings. No art, no humanity."

A burst of cheers and applause erupted. Rick took an elaborate bow and blew kisses.

"Wow! Good job, Rick and Team Three," Mrs. Wilkins said.

Oliver's cheeks burned as Rick bathed in the wild applause and lively praise.

11

Oliver dropped his keys on the desk, sunk low in his prison corner and buried his face with his hands.

What is wrong with me? Why does Rick hate me so much?

Tears swelled up, but Oliver forcibly clenched his fists and commanded himself not to cry.

Suddenly, he had an uncontrollable urge to go online to keep his mind off the bad. He uncurled from the fetal position, got up, and turned on the laptop.

Oliver hurriedly clicked on Surfer, typed in Two Cents, and noticed new updates from his class. He clicked on a thread titled "Rick the Hero" and witnessed floods of posts.

MightyMark: *Wow, Rick you are such a good public speaker.*

Eli101: *Where did you learn to speak like that?*

June: *I wish I could be as confident as you.*

SageForrest: *Nice going on carrying your team. Especially that clueless Oliver. How did he get accepted into that contest? It must be a mistake.*

Oliver tightly shut his eyes like a warehouse door locked down. *A mistake.*

After a while, he opened them up one at a time and the message still flashed back at him. He quickly slapped the laptop shut, clutched his keys, and departed to the elevators.

He pressed "G" for the ground floor. On floor three, the elevator stopped and a young girl got on. She donned a polka dot hat and carried a large pearl purse. They awkwardly exchanged glances as she pressed "G," even though it was already selected.

DING!

Oliver waited for the little girl to get off the elevator first and then followed suit. He dashed towards the security kiosk, pacing himself in the long, narrow, white corridor.

"Deputy Jerry!"

Oliver sprinted to the kiosk area where he was greeted by a confused looking Deputy Jerry.

"What's the matter, Oliver? You're huffing and puffing like you just ran a marathon."

"I'm TIRED! I'm FED UP! I can't stand my life anymore!"

"Do you want to talk inside the room?"

Oliver ignored his request. "Why do people hate me so much? I didn't do anything wrong to them. I didn't steal anything from them. I didn't hurt them. Why is it that my whole class hates me?!"

Several onlookers bulged with fright at Oliver's fit of temper.

"Now, I know you're upset and have a lot on your mind. But I'm going to need you to control your voice, Oliver. Can you do that for me?"

Oliver shivered and heaved his shoulders. After a few deep breaths, he steadied his voice. "Sorry, I'm just upset that Rick made me look bad today."

"Rick? Is this the same guy you were talking about earlier?"

"Yeah. Today, he did all the work on the assignment, and then when it came time for presentations, he forced me to present. When I didn't know what to say, he just took over and everyone loved it while I was left in the dust." Oliver crossed his arms and started hugging himself. "Why does he hate me so much?"

Deputy Jerry placed his hand on Oliver's shoulder. "I wish I could tell you why he's doing this. But I can't get inside his head. You have to talk to your teacher if things are getting out of hand."

"She can't do anything. She sees this happening in the class and let's it go," Oliver snapped.

"Well, then maybe try talking to him to see what's really going on. You really don't know what goes on behind closed doors. See if you can sit down and have a talk."

Oliver's eyeballs rolled back. *Yeah, right.*

Deputy Jerry drilled on. "I know it's difficult, but sometimes you have to be the bigger person. Can you do that?"

Oliver remained silent, staring at the ground. He didn't like the advice, but the sincerity in Deputy Jerry's voice lowered his guard.

"Think about it." He let go of his shoulder. "By the way, did you make it to the final round? I think I heard on the radio that the winners were contacted today," Deputy Jerry asked.

Oliver smacked his forehead. He forgot to check his email. The whole day has been a blur since the presentation. "Oh, I have to check."

"Well, go on!" Deputy Jerry's walkie-talkie emitted static noise. "It's DJ-400, what's going on? Noise on 14th floor? I'll be right on it."

Deputy Jerry placed his walkie-talkie back on his utility belt. "Sorry, Oliver. I have to run. Best of luck and remember, don't treat people as bad as they are. Treat them as good as you are." Deputy Jerry waved and zipped towards the elevator shaft.

44

A memory of Rick's smug face flashed into Oliver's mind. He shook it away as Oliver stood like a statue, trying to let Deputy Jerry's words sink in.

12

"**N**ext!"

The cafeteria ladies barked at the next wave of students as they slinked through the lunch line. The aroma of food reeked as each student robotically picked up a plastic tray, styrofoam plate and quilted napkins.

It was Toonie Taco Tuesday, but the only semblance to tacos was the name. The bread was extremely stiff and difficult to fold while the meat was vastly undercooked.

Oliver was next in line and handed over his plate to the cafeteria lady. In a swift motion, she grabbed the crusty taco bread, stuffed a handful of meat and returned the plate on Oliver's tray. "Next!"

Oliver carried his tray towards the main seating area and scanned the perimeter. The auburn tables were formed in clusters of three rows, and it was difficult to spot a lone table or chair. Students of various ages guffawed and engaged in all kinds of conversations.

After examining the area, Oliver finally spotted an isolated table far off in the right corner of the cafeteria. He scuttled there, passing by athletes, musicians, and anime groupies.

Oliver settled away from the ruckus and started chewing on his "taco." He winced as he bit into the stiff bread and hastily wiped his mouth with the napkin.

Suddenly, Oliver heard a loud howl from the middle of the cafeteria. Someone was jumping up and down ecstatically and making ear-splitting noises.

"I'm in the finals!" the voice cried. A few people clapped.

Oliver strained to see who caused the commotion. Before he could decipher who it was, the person zipped towards the front, bolted up onto the wooden stage and cupped both hands over his mouth. "I'm in the Write Speech finals! See you all from the top!"

Rick leaped off the stage, plonked down in the middle of the cafeteria and laughed uncontrollably.

Oliver gobbled down the remainder of his tortilla torture and grasped his tray to toss out the garbage. He sought after the route on the side aisles, but discovered the hassle to go through each person clogging up the sides.

Oliver decided to take the middle route. *Just ignore Rick. He probably won't even notice you.*

Oliver's eyes dipped down and quickly paced his steps towards the silver trash can. He pushed the moveable lid and deposited his plate in the garbage.

"Hey, Olive! Did you get to the finals?" Rick barked.

Oliver ignored him and darted towards the double doors on the side.

"Olive!" Rick's voice drowned in the sea of muttering conversations. Oliver's heart pounded as he burst through the doors. He was half-expecting Rick to follow him, but when he turned, Rick was nowhere to be seen.

Oliver noticed he was still gripping the cafeteria tray, but wasn't prepared to go back inside. Instead, he left it on the floor. *Someone will pick it up.*

Oliver roamed to the theatre room, his sanctuary. Normally, drama instructors held class in the morning, but it was usually empty during midday. Whenever Oliver had the chance, he visited this room and hung out by himself.

Oliver passed by a series of grey stained lockers. He was almost at the theatre room, tucked away at the corner of the school. Inspirational sayings and posters greeted him as he progressed.

"Express to impress."

"From invisible to visible."

"Why disguise when you can improvise?"

Oliver peered through the little glass on the door to determine if the room was occupied. *Empty.* Oliver turned the silver knob and eagerly walked in.

There was something magical about the high curtains, spotlight system and creaky hardwood floor. Oliver sat cross legged on his favourite spot: centre stage. He pulled out his laptop and turned it on.

After a minute, the proverbial "Welcome" message speckled the screen. Hunched over, Oliver logged into his email and came across a multitude of spam.

`Special deal on manicures!`

`Want to increase storage space on your computer?`

`Lose 10 pounds in 10 minutes!`

Oliver tediously deleted unsolicited messages until it got to the point of mind-numbing work. He almost obliterated another message until he carefully glanced at the subject heading: `Write Speech Audition`.

Oliver's bottom lip quivered a little. His finger grazed over the mouse touch pad and allowed the cursor to hover over the message for a while. With a deep breath, he clicked on the message. He compulsively bit his lip as he waited for the page to load.

Dear Oliver Masque.

Thank you for your video submission. We are writing to inform you that you have been selected to advance to the finals! Your video was heartfelt, sincere and demonstrated a genuine connection to the audience. Write Speech will arrange transportation for you to arrive at the Downtown Convention Centre. Once again, congratulations and please reply with your information below to register for transportation.

-Write Speech

Oliver fervently rubbed his eyes and moved his bewildered face closer to the laptop screen. He let out a cry of victory and started thrusting his fists in the air.

BRRING!

Oliver immediately paused halfway through his celebration and sheepishly smiled to himself. He packed up his laptop and grinned his whole way out of the sanctuary.

13

I' *m in the finals.*

Oliver kept repeating that to himself, struggling to internalize this revelation. The autumn leaves sporadically drifted to the ground and created a beautiful pattern of yellow, red and green.

Oliver let his feet have a mind of their own. He was brought to a halt at the intersection, waiting for the pedestrian light to flare.

The pudgy crossing guard detected Oliver's upbeat behaviour. "Nice day."

"Yeah, it's nice." Oliver nodded.

"Listen to this joke I found: 'What did the tree say to autumn? Leaf me alone!' "

Oliver politely smiled as she guffawed.

The pedestrian sign flashed green and the crossing guard made her way in front of Oliver. "You have yourself a good one, kiddo."

"You too!"

Oliver practically sprinted to the vestibule of his apartment. A lady with a canary yellow hat exited at the moment Oliver arrived. She held the door open for a few seconds as he breathily expressed his thanks. He fumbled around with the key in his pocket and pulled it out. He inserted it into the lock and paraded his way to the elevator.

Oliver gleefully pressed the button repeatedly but then stopped and glanced sideways.

Wait until Deputy Jerry hears this!

Oliver marched to the kiosk and persistently tapped on the glass window.

A large, burly security guard loomed into view. His tree trunk neck had a pulsating vein. His golden badge featured prominently on his right pocket.

"Yes?"

"Hi, can I speak with Deputy Jerry?" Oliver beamed.

"He's not in right now."

"Oh." Oliver dropped his shoulders. "Do you know when he'll be back?"

"Can't say for sure. Check back later."

"Okay, thank you."

Suddenly, a new idea popped into his head. *Dr. Hailey Bell!*

Oliver started tapping his foot impatiently. At last, the elevator arrived and he hopped on. He pressed "5" and immediately pressed the button to close the doors quicker.

"Wait!"

A scrawny guy rushed towards the elevators just as the tanned doors were closing in. Oliver witnessed him running but was tardy to release the doors in time. The elevator slammed in the poor guy's face.

Oliver stared at the ceiling mirror as the elevator made its way up. He dusted off a couple specks from his autumn jacket and pushed his hair away from his face.

DING!

Oliver stood in front of room 500 and knocked on the door. No reply. He knocked harder, but still nothing.

Looks like she's not home.

With a defeated sigh, Oliver turned and dawdled back to

the elevator shaft. After taking a few steps, he heard the sound of a door unlocking.

"Oliver! Sorry I didn't answer before. I was cooking and the stove fan was making a loud noise." Dr. Bell exclaimed.

"Dr. Bell, I made it!" Oliver said.

Dr. Bell's forehead crinkled into a mystified expression, but tried to match Oliver's cheeriness. "That's great, Oliver! Pardon me, but what did you make?"

"I'm in the finals of the Write Speech competition! I got the confirmation email and they said they're taking care of transportation." Oliver's eyes shined like quarters.

Dr. Bell's eyes widened and she clapped her hands together. "Wow! Congratulations, Oliver! Did you try the tea I gave you? Did it help?"

Oliver's head bobbled up and down.

"Glad to hear it. Wow, you must be so happy. Your family must be really proud of you." Dr. Bell smiled.

Family.

The word stung Oliver. He pursed his lips into a smile and said, "Yeah, they're really supportive."

"Wonderful. Would you like to come inside? I'm making pancakes," Dr. Bell said.

"Sure."

Oliver stepped inside room 500 and gracefully removed his shoes. Dr. Bell put out fresh plates with pancakes on them. He hungrily shovelled the flat delight as if his stomach was a bottomless pit. She chuckled to herself at Oliver's appetite.

When he finished, Oliver waved goodbye and trotted his way up to his apartment.

He laid on the floor of his living room, arms crossed behind his head with nonstop thoughts racing through his mind. He imagined winning first place, shaking hands with the emcee and experiencing the deafening applause. Most of all, he desired to see Rick's smug smile wiped off his face.

Can't wait.

After some time, Oliver stood up and changed into his pyjamas. He decided to get a good night's rest before planning preparations for the competition. He almost crawled into bed but noticed the prestigious pen lying on the far end of the desk. He picked it up and cradled it in his hands.

It all started with this.

He gently set it down and shifted his gaze towards the framed note with his name etched in front. Oliver lifted up the frame, gave it a small kiss and set it down.

I'm getting closer.

14

Dear Write Speech finalist,

Congratulations once again on making it this far! This is a wonderful opportunity to showcase your public speaking abilities and to take audiences on a journey with your words. Here are the details of the competition.

Theme: Helping Humanity Holistically

Speech Length: 10 minutes

Dress code: Business Formal

Location: Downtown Convention Centre

Date: October 27

Registration: starts at 4:00 p.m.

Your objective is to deliver a speech in line with that theme. It could range from homelessness to mental health. It's up to you what message you feel humanity needs to hear! We are expecting a crowd of approximately 5,000 attendees. If you have any questions, comments or concerns, feel free to send a message through our live chat.

-Write Speech

Oliver carefully read the latest Write Speech email and a burst of ideas formed in his head. *Health? Friendship? Technology?*

Oliver explored the internet for strategies on how to pick a winning speech topic. An overwhelming 30 million recommendations of articles flashed back at his face.

"Hot Topics for Speeches."

"How NOT to bore your audience."

"Razzle and Dazzle with the right speech."

Oliver was intrigued at the "Hot Topics for Speeches" article; the latest trends seemed to be a good place to start. The website showcased a short, bullet point list of promising subjects including leadership, family, economics and virtual reality.

Oliver scanned through the list, and to his disappointment, didn't find a walkthrough on how to select the right speech topic. Before he clicked away, a bright "Bonus Tip" graphic appeared on the centre of the screen.

`Make sure you dress to impress. You don't get a second chance at a first impression.`

Oliver swung his restless gaze at what he was wearing: a faded blue t-shirt and jeans ripped at the knees.

I need a suit.

Oliver stood up and wandered over to his closet. He pulled open the sliding doors and sifted through his inventory. Jackets, shirts and jeans. Not a single, complete formal attire.

How am I supposed to afford a fancy suit?

Oliver sat back at the laptop and clicked on the "Live Chat" link at the bottom of the Write Speech email. A new window emerged which took up half his screen. The Write Speech logo filled the top and there was space to type out the chat.

POP!

Hi, this is Andrea from Write Speech. How may I help you?

Oliver cracked his fingers. This was his time to shine.

Hi, I'm Oliver Masque, a Write Speech finalist. Do you know where I can rent a suit? I'm a student, so money is a bit tight.

Oliver sent the message, but immediately regretted it. *You doofus! Why did you write that you can't afford a suit? Now, she's probably going to think I'm some lazy idiot who can't get a job.*

The customer service agent typed her reply. It seemed to take forever to get a response. Oliver anxiously waited as he stared at the pervaded message: Andrea is typing...

After twenty seconds of agonizing wait for a reply, Oliver contemplated clicking away. Perhaps he embarrassed himself, and by closing the chat, he could start over again with someone new.

POP!

Congratulations on being a finalist, Oliver! Write Speech is a proud affiliate of Taylored Suits. Since you are a student and a finalist, you can get a 50% discount on all three piece suits and accessories. Use the promo code WSPEECH to get the discount. Is there anything else I can do for you, Oliver?

Oliver sat stunned for a few seconds. He fixated on the "50% discount" but quickly shook himself out of a trance and began typing.

-Thank you so much! That's all I needed.

-My pleasure, Oliver. Good luck at the competition.

He quickly typed in "Taylored Suits" in the search engine.

Please, don't be too far.

To Oliver's delight, there was a branch right in the shopping mall near his apartment. Even though he visited the mall countless times for grocery shopping or other errands, he didn't pay much attention to clothing stores. He didn't think he would ever be in the company of important people.

Oliver ditched his speech topic research and read up on basic knowledge about the essentials of suit shopping.

After a few minutes of browsing various websites, Oliver grew in confidence. *Make sure the sleeves go down to the wrist. Measure your neck size so you can wear dress shirts that are accustomed to it. Make sure the material fits your body type, not too tight and not too loose. Wear a pocket square to complete the look.*

Oliver grabbed a piece of scrap paper and scribbled the tips down as fast as he could. He lingered over the notes once more, to see if anything was missing. *This should be good for now.* He folded the paper in half and placed it in his left jeans back pocket.

He turned off the laptop, grabbed his wallet and headed out the door. The mall was within walking distance and Oliver intended to make a stellar payment.

15

The golden Taylored Suits sign shined brilliantly against the black marble backdrop. Oliver hovered outside the enchanting store, mesmerized by the aura of prestige. There were mannequins on either side of the main entrance displaying tuxedos, three-piece suits and other business attires.

The main entryway was encrusted with gold paint and featured a glossy, wavy design. Oliver soothingly touched the gold and stepped inside.

"Why, hello, young man! Welcome to Taylored Suits!"

His jet black hair was slicked back and he had a finely trimmed pencil moustache. His copper coloured three-piece suit matched his classy dress shoes. The man's plastered smile resembled the mannequins' gleeful expressions.

"My name is Taylor from, well, you guessed it, Taylored Suits. What can I do for you, sir?"

"H-hi. I'm Oliver," Oliver extended his hand.

"It's an absolute pleasure to meet and serve you, Oliver." Taylor grasped his hand, moved it up and down with five solid pumps, and let go.

"So, what are you looking for?"

"Actually, I'm a finalist for the Write Speech competition and I-"

Taylor's eyes widened. "You're a finalist? Congratulations! Wow, that's amazing!"

"Y-yes, thank you. I'm a student and n-need help renting out a suit for the competition."

Taylor held his smooth palms up. "Say no more. I've got just the one for you. Follow me."

Taylor roamed towards the middle of the store and Oliver obediently followed. Ties of various patterns racked up across the wall. A large, pink "50% off" sign written with black permanent marker was placed in the center of a circular hanger carrying blazers.

"This just came in last week. I think you were born to wear it. It's made from wool. Go on, feel the texture. It's European." Taylor added with a smile.

Oliver used his left forefinger and thumb to feel the stone coloured suit. "It's nice, but no offense, it seems a bit too plain."

Taylor was perplexed. "What do you mean?"

Oliver let go of the suit sleeve and stared at Taylor. "I want a suit that will really catch people's attention. Something that will make them really notice me."

"Alright, let's see what we have that will dazzle your audience, Mr. Public Speaker." Taylor tapped his chin and glanced around the store. "Ah, I know! Maybe this will work. Wait right here."

Taylor vanished while Oliver patiently stayed. He was in awe at the vast array of charcoal grey, sandy brown, wool navy suit selection.

After a few moments, Taylor re-appeared in front of Oliver with a shiny blazer. "This will definitely turn some heads. Put it on."

Oliver slipped into the silver blazer. The smooth polyester texture grazed his skin. He adjusted the collar and asked,

"How do I look?"

"See for yourself." He pointed to a full length mirror situated on a nearby column.

Oliver steadily walked up to it and outstretched his arms to check if the suit was too small. He turned around, but just enough so he could turn his head back to the mirror.

"It's better, but I think it's a bit too much. The shininess I mean," Oliver sighed.

Taylor's jaw clenched slightly while grinding his teeth. "Not a problem. How about this: you look around the store and if you find something you like, give me a shout."

"Okay, but I don't think I can yell that loud."

"It's just a saying, Oliver. It's-never mind. Here, let me take that from you." Taylor motioned towards the silver suit. Oliver handed it over to him and Taylor quickly retreated to the corner of the store.

Oliver was left alone and circled around, eyeing all the different departments to see which suit was "The One." Some were too large, others were too expensive, even with the discount code.

Looks like there's nothing here for me.

With his shoulders hunched over, Oliver slowly moped his way out of the store. *Maybe this is a sign. Maybe I'm not meant to be on stage.*

Just as he was about to step outside, Oliver halted. A glimpse of an oddly, bright red blazer drew him in with long, quick strides.

Oliver yanked it from underneath the pile, and the neatly stacked assortment turned into a disheveled mess. He held the fiery red blazer with both hands and couldn't stop staring at it. The colour was just perfect, bright, but not blinding. The texture was just perfect, handmade, but not itchy. The size was just perfect, slim fit, but not tight.

This is it!

Oliver galloped around the store in search of Taylor. He found him assorting ties in a "T" shape on the wall. "Sir, I found it!"

Taylor stopped arranging the ties. "Wow, you have an interesting taste. That blazer is actually on sale because we've been trying to sell that thing for months and no one has ever wanted it."

Oliver's eyes glimmered. "I'm certain, this is the right one for me."

Taylor rubbed the back of his neck. "Okay, if you say so. I'll go to the back and get the matching pants, vest and shirt." He took a few steps, and turned around.

"By the way, please forgive me if I sounded harsh beforehand. Let me make it up to you. You said you were a student, right? I'll also throw in a complementary shoe rental for a price you can't refuse. Let me go to the back and get the matching pieces and I'll ring up the purchase."

Taylor marched to the back of the store where it said, "Employees Only."

Oliver glanced down at the red blazer and smiled. The unwanted blazer found its new home.

16

Oliver's stomach growled like a territorial crocodile. The gold coloured trim on the handles sparkled as he strolled past the various stores.

The food court was packed with unruly toddlers in high chairs, and mothers dreadfully attempting to feed them.

Oliver glanced around, squeezed past a family of five and lurched to a vacant table. He was a few steps to securing his spot, but stopped in his tracks.

I can't just leave my stuff here while I go order.

Disgruntled, Oliver abandoned the space and marched towards the Guzzling Grubs lineup station.

He dropped his bags as he glanced at the menu's infographic above the cashiers. He glossed over the Wrecked Wrap for $3, complete with powerful pita bread, mixed in with tumbling turnips, perfect pickles, tummy tomatoes and great garlic sauce.

"Can I help the next person in line?"

Ahead of Oliver was an elderly gentleman with an unbelievably shiny, bald head. His blue checkered shirt looked like a racing flag. Oliver moved up closer as the man limped forward to the cashier.

"Gimmie a Solid Salad," the man ordered.

"Sure, is there anything else you'd like?"

"Ummmm, let me see," he squinted at the menu. "What's that Super Splash drink you got 'dere?"

"It's a tropical fruit mix drink."

"Ummmm, let me see," the man pulled out his aged wallet

and fussily counted coins. "You know, these days you can't get your money's worth. Back in my day..."

Oliver's stomach growled again and placed agitated hands on his waist.

Finally, the man finished his order and Oliver moved up. He slid his bags and let out an exasperated sigh. "Whew! Can I get a Wrecked Wrap?"

"Sure. Anything else?" the lady asked flatly.

"No."

"That'll be $3. Paper or plastic?"

After the transaction and a few minutes of unbearable waiting, Oliver received his wrap in a paper bag and assessed the likelihood of an empty seating spot.

Great, no more spaces.

Holding the wrap in one hand and the bags with the other, Oliver darted through the crowd of people. He hoped for a miracle that someone will coincidentally get up and give their spot to Oliver.

A man's shiny head popped up like a gopher and noticed Oliver wearily searching for a spot. Bits of food soared from his mouth as he yelled, "Please sit here!"

Oliver disgustedly glanced back at the waving man with the familiar shiny head. His vision scoured the area, desperate for another spot.

After unsuccessfully locating a seat, Oliver reluctantly moved to the eager man's table. He set his bags on the floor and unraveled the Wrecked Wrap. He devoured it with a giant chomp and the great garlic sauce melted in his mouth.

"My, my quite hungry, are we?" the bald man flashed a

huge smile. He had a silver tooth, which was partially covered with parsley.

Oliver glared at him. "Yeah," he mumbled as garlic sauce dribbled down his chin.

After chomping down on his sandwich and wiping his face with a napkin, he pulled out his stocky, slightly outdated phone. Oliver seldom used it except for important matters. He connected it to "Food Court Wi-Fi" and searched for tips on deciding speech topics. He scrolled through a list of questions every public speaker should ask.

What do you know about? Who is your audience? Why are you speaking in the first place?

Oliver read through each question and then grunted loudly out of frustration.

"What's the matter, sonny boy?" the bald man asked, sucking his teeth.

Oliver's eyes flickered up from his phone. "It's nothing."

"Come, now. That grunt sounded like something I heard in the woods once. What's eating you?"

Oliver sighed. "I'm making a speech and don't know what to say."

"Ah, a public speaker! I've done quite a few speeches back in my day as a history teacher. It's fun, let me tell you."

Oliver sensed that the old man was gearing up for a lengthy speech, so he quickly picked up his bags and stuffed his phone in his pocket. "Sorry, but I have to get going now."

The old man's eyes slanted like a gloomy pup. "No problem, young lad. You go off and give an amazing speech. Where is it held?"

"It's the Write Speech conference." Oliver packed up his bags, turned and started to walk away.

"Remember, a speech from the heart reaches hearts."

Oliver paused. He blinked and glanced back at the bald man. His silver tooth's metallic luster glistened like the sparkles on an ocean.

17

"**I**'m going to split up the class into two teams."
Mrs. Wilkins positioned herself in the centre of the room and keenly outstretched her arm. "Everyone on my left is a team and everyone on my right is the other team."

Classmates briefly exchanged looks with one another. Oliver was on the far right. Rick was in the far left.

"What are we doing, Miss?" Rick snarled.

Mrs. Wilkins held up a finger. "Just a second. I'm going to explain in a moment. Does everyone know what team they're on?"

Silence.

"Okay, good. Here's how this game will work. I'll be asking questions about art and the first team to get three questions right wins. No notes." Mrs. Wilkins glanced at a student opening up her binder with loose papers.

"Now, we need leaders to call out the answers on behalf of the teams. Who wants to-"

Rick's hand shot up. "I'm the captain of this ship!"

"Wonderful, Rick. How about Team Two?"

Silence.

"We need to select a leader so we can get started," Mrs. Wilkins said firmly.

Oliver stood up. "I'll be the team leader."

Team Two fixated their stares in shock while Mrs. Wilkins smiled. "That's great, Oliver!"

Rick dubiously glared at Oliver and Oliver returned the glare while sitting down.

"First question is for Team One. Oh, by the way, if a team doesn't get the answer correctly, it goes to the other team. Alright, question one: 'What do you call the irrational juxtaposing of images?' "

Rick stayed silent for a few seconds, rubbing his chin. "Hmmm, is it Surrealism?"

Mrs. Wilkins was thunderstruck. "Wow! Yes, that's right, Rick. Next time, try consulting with your teammates before blurting out answers."

"Don't worry, Miss. I'll lead my team to victory," Rick sneered.

Mrs. Wilkins' heels clattered as she proceeded to the chalkboard and crisply wrote the headers "Team One" and "Team Two." The chalk smoothly grazed the board as she drew a large checkmark under the column of Team One. She cheerfully turned towards the other half of the class.

"Which Shakespearean play inspired the quote, 'The object of art is to give life a shape?' Isn't that a nice quote?" Mrs. Wilkins grinned.

Oliver scratched his head, then surveyed his teammates. "What do you all think?"

There was a feeble attempt at brainstorming answers with his nonchalant and distant peers.

"You're the leader. Just say something," Caroline said, scrunching up her pink frames.

Oliver was appalled. *No one respects me.*

"Umm, is it *Macbeth*?" Oliver asked.

"Oh, no. Sorry Team Two, that answer is incorrect. Team One is going for the steal," Mrs. Wilkins said with a slight bit of excitement in her voice.

"It's *A Midsummer Night's Dream*," Rick immediately replied.

Mrs. Wilkins sighed at her failed attempt for cohesive collaboration. "Yes, that's correct."

She made her way to the blackboard and drew another checkmark beside the one drawn previously.

"Team Two, you need make a huge comeback in order to stay in the game. Focus and put all your efforts together. Your next question is this: 'The *Ships and Arches* painting is an example of...?' "

Oliver stared at his teammates and they were coldly staring at him back, shrugging shoulders and waiting for his response.

Ships and Arches is about deceptive senses. It looks like one thing, but the brain interprets another.

Oliver took a deep breath. "Is the answer Optical Illusion?" He shut his eyes and waited for the rejection.

Mrs. Wilkins smiled. "That's correct!" She cheerfully trotted over to the blackboard and outlined a giant checkmark underneath the Team Two column.

Oliver opened one eye at a time. He sat up a bit straighter.

"Team One: 'This technical term means a thing which has height, weight and depth.' " Mrs. Wilkins asked.

Rick blurted out, "That's Perspective!"

Mrs. Wilkins solemnly shook her head. "That's incorrect. Team Two for the steal?"

A few students glared angrily at Rick. "Why didn't you wait for us?! What's the matter with you?"

"Settle down, settle down!" Mrs. Wilkins waved her hands up and down. Finally, the chatter dwindled to a frustrated silence.

"Team Two?"

Oliver hesitated. "Is that...form?" He shut his eyes again.

Mrs. Wilkins beamed. "Right, again!" She pranced to the chalkboard, and in a swift motion, drew a lovely checkmark. "Now that things are tied, this final question will determine the winner."

Rick was fidgeting in his chair, anxious to continue. "Hurry up! What's the next question?"

Mrs. Wilkins pressed her lips tightly. "Team One: 'Between the 15th and 17th centuries, it was considered ideal to be known as a Renaissance man or Renaissance woman. What is another term associated with that in modern times?' "

Rick raised his hand. "Oh! Oh! It's a polygon!"

Suddenly, a wave of exasperated sighs filled the room.

"Are you kidding me?"

"Polygon is for geometry, doofus."

Mrs. Wilkins hushed the angry protests. She turned to face Oliver. "What is Team Two's answer?"

Oliver's palms started sweating buckets. His teammates were now observing him, but more warmly this time. "I think it's called a poly-something," one of his teammates said.

"Yeah, I think so too," another teammate chimed in.

Oliver thought for another moment and a light bulb went off in his head.

"It's Polymath!" Oliver proclaimed.

Mrs. Wilkins smiled from ear to ear. "Team Two is the

winner!" She made her way to the blackboard and made a third checkmark, happily marking the column with a bold "Winner" label.

Team Two erupted in cheers and applause. Oliver's cheeks burned red as a few compliments were directed his way.

"Nice going, Oliver!"

"You came in clutch!"

"Amazing dude!"

Oliver basked in glory while Rick stared coldly, with his arms tightly crossed with fisted hands.

18

THUMP.

Oliver carelessly slid off his backpack and it landed on the apartment floor. He jittered with glee as he sat on the bed, replaying the latest class activity in his mind. Oliver wasn't used to people saying nice things, or even being acknowledged.

Today was a good day.

The icing on the cake was seeing Rick's frustrated face. Oliver savoured the aggravation and wished he could have a photo to capture that moment forever.

Oliver dug out a scrap piece of paper from his backpack and sat down on his desk. His left arm outstretched for the elegant pen and clasped it tightly. He stared at the paper for a second and then, the words came pouring out of him. Oliver continued to write and write until he reached the bottom of the page. When he was done, he exhaled deeply and read it over:

Dear Me,

Today was probably the best day of my life. For once, people acknowledged me and actually said nice things. It was an art class with Mrs. Wilkins and there were two teams. When no one else said anything, I stepped up and became the team leader. It was scary, but I did it! Our team was down 0-2 and we had to answer 3 straight. We won, but more importantly, Rick lost. I will forever remember this day.

From,

Me

Oliver read it over one more time, folded up the endearing letter and placed it in the upper drawer of his desk. He felt elated, but unsure of what to do with himself.

He flipped open his laptop and waited for the screen to load. Oliver pulled open the drawer and read the letter again until the Welcome screen appeared. He set down the letter, and with a few clicks, entered Two Cents.

An unusually large message took up the front page.

> WRITE SPEECH COMPETITION HAPPENING THIS WEEKEND!
>
> LOCAL NEWS STATIONS ARE SEARCHING FOR CONTESTANTS TO CONDUCT INTERVIEWS.
>
> IF YOU ARE A CONTESTANT, MESSAGE HERE.
>
> -VORTEX NEWS

Oliver's bony jaw dropped. The local city news station was on the lookout for him.

He hastily clicked on the Vortex News username, clicked on the enormous, red pencil icon and started composing his message.

Hi Vortex News,
My name is Oliver and I'm a contestant...

Oliver realized he was sending the message anonymously. His fingers trembled and he froze in place.

Maybe if I just explain who I am in the message, they'll realize it's me.

But he second guessed himself. Anyone can be anonymous and claim to be him. *Why should they believe me?*

Oliver started to panic as thoughts were racing a mile a minute. *What if people find out about my account? What if there's a chance they could say mean things directly? What if...*

The doubts overpowered him and Oliver started to feel drained. He buried his face and felt his intestines violently clench. The gentle whir from his laptop fan alleviated the silence.

Oliver remained paralyzed with fear until the burst of positive remarks rushed back to his head. *My classmates recognized me.*

He snapped fully alert and energetically pounded his fist onto the desk. *I will make that account.*

Oliver exited the composed message and navigated back to the front page of Two Cents. He discovered the "New Account" button and once clicked, an unfamiliar blue form appeared. It asked for a username, password, address and other basic information.

Let's do this.

Oliver meticulously filled in the details, and decided to label his username "OliverMasque." Once the form was complete and approved, he heaved a sigh of relief. *That's it. I'm open to the public now.*

He retraced his steps back to the Vortex News mailbox and formulated his new message:

```
Hi Vortex News,

This is Oliver Masque, a finalist for the
Write Speech competition. I would love to have
```

an interview. Please, let me know how this will be conducted.

Oliver pressed the "Send" button and waited a few minutes. Remarkably, he got a speedy reply.

Dear Oliver,

That's wonderful! Just for verification purposes, could you send a copy of the message saying you are a finalist?

-Write Speech

Oliver immediately logged into his email, found the acceptance message and copy/pasted into the reply composition in Two Cents.

Thank you, Oliver! Do you have a webcam? If so, we are scheduled to have the Write Speech segment at 10:00 a.m. tomorrow. The link to enter our newsroom is below. Please confirm if this works with you.

-Write Speech

Oliver hovered over the link. He softly grazed the built-in laptop webcam and contemplated using his mediocre camera. *What other choice do I have? It's not like I can just go buy a new one.*

-Yes, I have a webcam and 10:00 a.m. works with me.

-Great! See you tomorrow.

As Oliver signed off, it dawned on him that this was his first ever interview.

19

9:30 a.m. Thirty measly minutes to get ready.

Oliver incessantly scratched his eyebrow while reaching in his dingy refrigerator. A half-opened packet of one-minute noodles sat innocently on the top shelf. He hungrily pulled it out and shut the door.

Oliver boiled a cup of limp noodles and continuously stirred with a fork. Once the meal was ready, he prepared the squiggly delight on the table and brought it to his mouth.

"Ouch!" He rushed to the sink and ran cold water from the tap. Oliver lowered his head and lapped water into his mouth with his burnt tongue. After a few rounds, he stopped and headed back to the table.

When it finally cooled down, Oliver loudly slurped the soul food and glanced at the stove clock.

9:45 a.m.

Oliver's eyes widened as he shovelled noodles into his cheeks. He nearly choked as he wolfed down another mouthful and swallowed.

Fiercely patting his chest, Oliver sprinted to the bedroom. He stumbled over to his closet and saw the winter white dress shirt, a torn grey t-shirt, a baggy brown sweater and a bee-striped shirt. He selected the dress shirt and buttoned it all the way to the top.

He quickly booted up the laptop and logged into Two Cents.

9:56 a.m.

He clicked on the Vortex News link and the screen

buffered. Oliver adjusted the webcam, rustled his hair and tried to coax himself down. The link opened up and he was on "Standby."

Oliver's ringed hazel pupils stared intently at the laptop timer, carefully watching the digits change incrementally.

Once the timer hit 10:00 a.m., a large window appeared. It was the news anchor, and Oliver's window minimized to the top left corner of the screen.

"Our next guest is a finalist from the anticipated Write Speech competition. Welcome, Oliver!" the news anchor said.

Oliver sat there open mouthed. He quickly closed it up and cleared his throat of the sticky phlegm. "H-hi."

"Tell us, what inspired you to take place in this competition?"

Oliver rubbed his neck. "Well, it's kind of a long story. I actually didn't want to do it at first, but a friend really encouraged me to try."

"That's the shortest long story I've ever heard," the news anchor chuckled.

Oliver joined in with nervous laughter. "Yeah, I guess."

"So, aren't you afraid of public speaking? I mean it's one of the highest phobias that people have. Do you have nerves of steel?"

Oliver gulped. "Actually, I'm scared. Terrified, really."

A thick silence settled over them. The news anchor shifted her glance and was about to fill the void, but Oliver pressed on.

"But, it's just something I want to do. I-I think it's possible."

"Very inspirational, Oliver. Now, we only have time for one

more question: if you could give advice to the thousands of viewers here today, what would it be?"

Oliver paused for a few seconds. *Thousands of viewers?* "Uhhh...be yourself?"

The news anchor wore a disappointed, scowling expression on her face. "I see. Thank you for joining us today, Oliver."

Oliver gave a slight nod and awkwardly waved.

"We are continuing our segments with the Write Speech competitors right after the break, so stay tuned."

Oliver turned off his webcam and sat like a tree fixed in its place. *Thousands of viewers?!*

Oliver's mind buzzed as the live stream switched to a commercial of scissors slicing through various packages of unhealthy foods. The tagline read "Cut Out Junk."

Oliver mentally checked out through the advertisements. He slouched in his chair like wilted grass under a potted plant.

"Welcome back to this segment on Vortex News. I'm here with finalists of the Write Speech competition to discuss their thoughts."

Oliver bolted back to life and concentrated on the interviewees. *Jeff seems smart. Holly has a great presence. Rob is really confident.*

Oliver perched his head on his right hand and it felt as heavy as an anchor.

"Now, let's welcome Rick."

Oliver suddenly perked up.

"It's a great pleasure being here today." Rick wore a white collared shirt with a cyan blue vest.

"What's your philosophy on public speaking?"

"You know, it's funny that people don't talk about public speaking, yet we have to do it on a daily basis. I look at public speaking as a way to verbalize thoughts, communicate ideas and consider it the ultimate form of expression." Rick answered.

"Fair enough. Why do you think public speaking isn't something discussed on a wider scale?"

Rick held his hands out in front of him. "I personally think it's about the intense fear of judgement and lack of developing that skill. Look, if people didn't constantly put down others when they have the mic, I think society would be more receptive towards public speaking. I mean, I always treat people with the utmost respect."

Oliver's tired eyes rolled skyward.

"At the end of the day, it's all about you. Imagine the kind of community we would have if more people stepped up and delivered compassionate speeches." Rick folded his arms.

"Wow, impressive responses! Looking forward to seeing how you do in the competition next weekend. All the best," the news anchor said.

"Thank you, Vortex News."

Oliver turned off the laptop, right at the moment where Rick smirked.

20

The sound of lockers slamming, students chattering, and shoes squeaking pervaded the high school. Oliver roamed through the hallways, a few minutes before art class began.

Along the way, he noticed joyful chatters subsiding whenever Oliver passed by. He was taken aback by the ominous occurrence. People stared and the thoughts of being negatively judged filled Oliver's mind.

He swung open the stair door and as he turned at the top, more strangers started staring at him. *What's going on?*

He entered the classroom with a perplexed expression. Mrs. Wilkins was preparing sheets and Rick engaged in idle activity. Just as he sat down, the speakers screeched.

"Good morning, students! Please, rise for the national anthem."

Oliver and his classmates collectedly stood up. Some students played with their phones while the national anthem commenced. Mrs. Wilkins proudly placed her hand over her heart.

"Thank you. Please, be seated. We have a lot of fun announcements for you today!"

Oliver tuned out the eerily cheerful voice. He only caught snippets regarding a food drive, basketball tryouts and cancellations for a games club meeting.

"Lastly, the Write Speech competition is this weekend and we're proud to have Rick Chaser and Oliver Masque from Mrs. Wilkins art class take part. They were on Vortex News yesterday. Good luck you two and have a dazzling day everyone!" The intercom signed out.

Oliver snapped awake. Rick merrily pumped his right fist in the air. Mrs. Wilkins nodded and smiled.

That's why people were staring. Maybe they saw the news segment.

Oliver started to sink into his chair like quicksand. *Now, lots of people know about this competition.*

"Wasn't that nice? Rick and Oliver were mentioned on the announcements. I'm so happy for the both of you." Mrs. Wilkins clapped.

Oliver and Rick exchanged glances from the corners of the room. Rick made a thumbs-down motion, but Oliver paid no heed.

"Before we review for the test next week, I have a proposal for you all." Mrs. Wilkins rubbed her hands together and grinned.

The students' muttering quieted down. Their laser focus on Mrs. Wilkins excited her.

"Since this weekend is going to be a busy one for Oliver and Rick, if you attend the Write Speech competition to show your support, I will give you a 10% bonus mark." Mrs. Wilkins approached the dusty blackboard and illustrated a number "10," outlined with a five-pointed star.

Classmates started whispering positively about the proposal. Mrs. Wilkins' eyes crinkled as the corners of her mouth turned up. "It looks like everyone is happy with the idea."

Her emerald glare locked onto Oliver, and then Rick. "I'll be at the competition rooting for you guys."

Rick jumped up out of his seat, "I'm gonna win!"

Oliver zipped his lips like a padlock.

"That's very nice, Rick. Please sit so we can get started on our review. Let's open our textbooks and turn to page 155."

The whole class will be there? What have I gotten myself into?

Oliver buried his head in his textbook. *What if I mess up? What if I forget my lines? Everyone will be there live and see it.*

He continuously plucked little pieces of hair as the psychological torture droned on throughout the whole period.

BRRING!

"Oliver?"

Mrs. Wilkins hovered over him. Her emerald green eyes bulged with concern. "Did you follow along with the test review?"

Oliver raised his head from the textbook and swept off the stray hairs from the pages. "Y-Yes, Mrs. Wilkins."

She could sense the quiver in his voice. "If you need anything, just ask. Looking forward to your speech!" She did a tiny wave and exited the class.

Oliver shook his head and began packing things up. He leaned over to jam his binder in the backpack.

"Hello, Olive."

Oliver tried to pry his eyes off his menacing gaze, continuing to pack his belongings.

"What's wrong? Aren't you going to say hi back? I just wanted to wish you good luck for the competition." Rick smiled.

Oliver stopped. *Is this a trick?*

Rick extended his right hand for a handshake and held it

out. Instantly, the throbbing pain vividly burned in Oliver's memory.

"Come on. May the best person win."

Maybe he changed.

Oliver extended his arm for the handshake, but brought it to a halt.

"How come you're being nice?" Oliver asked.

"Would you get on with it, Olive? I don't have all day. Are you going to shake my hand or not?"

Oliver stared at his own hand then proceeded to lock into a white-knuckle handshake. Immediately, Rick tightened his bone-crushing grip and Oliver succumbed to the all-too-familiar throbbing pain. Rick viciously slapped the back of Oliver's head with his other hand.

"You forgot something."

The force of the 300-page projectile slammed right in Oliver's face. He doubled over, with his nose rapidly swelling.

"I'm the next Write Speech champion." Rick arrogantly stepped on Oliver's textbook and let out a jarring laugh.

21

Oliver finished buttoning up his fresh, white shirt. His hazel eyes were fixated on his reflection. *October 27. Today is the big day.*

He grabbed his red tie from his bathroom counter and smoothly caressed it. The polyester material felt so smooth between his fingers.

How did that guy in the video tutorial do it again?

Oliver thought for a moment then placed the tie on his neck. He positioned it so that the longer, wide side fell lower than the thinner side. Then, he twisted it around, hooked it underneath the neck loop and tightened the Windsor knot.

Success.

Next, he grabbed his fiery red pants from the counter and slid it up one leg at a time. Oliver clipped on the metal harness and zipped up. He glanced down at his feet. *Just the right length.*

At last, the dashing blazer. Its radiating red brilliance made Oliver smile. He seized it from the door hanger and stuck his right arm through, followed by the left. They slid through the frictionless material like melted butter. Oliver compulsively adjusted his collar and stared at himself in the mirror for a moment, admiring his important appearance.

Oliver was tapping his chin. Something felt missing to him. He sauntered over to his bedroom to locate the original packaging. *A-ha, there it is.*

Included in the boxed shirt set was a premium pocket square. It was the magnetic type, which enhanced the professional look. He went back to the bathroom with the cream coloured, wooden pocket square.

He positioned it on the left, chest blazer pocket and carefully lined it up along the edge. Then, he placed the circular magnetic piece behind it and clipped right in place.

The shoes were next in line. The shiny, black leather sparkled. He bent down, slightly wiggled his toes and placed his thumb on the back to slide his shoes on each foot. He admired the sparkly jewels on his feet.

I'm ready.

Oliver shuffled to his bedroom and grasped the framed note on the desk. He speedily unscrewed the plastic backside and removed the sealed white envelope. Oliver devotedly placed the treasured possession in his jacket pocket and tenderly patted it.

He began to anxiously pace back and forth like a leopard in its cage. Oliver kept whipping out his chunky phone, checking to see new messages, and returning it in his hip pocket.

Suddenly, a spicy aroma filled Oliver's nostrils. He galloped to the kitchenette and poured himself a steamy waterfall of ginger tea. Once it cooled down, he clasped the mug with his right hand and slowly slurped the tea.

He stared off into space and pictured his classmates' reactions. Oliver imagined all kinds of possible scenarios, from thunderous applause to downright boredom. He envisioned the scenes in his head as the wave of ginger travelled down his esophagus. In the midst of his mental immersion, a random flash of a security badge and "Voice 4 You" sign popped up.

Deputy Jerry and Dr. Bell.

He was so caught up with the competition that he hadn't seen them for a while.

Oliver dropped the half-finished mug onto the table and double-checked his pockets: keys, phone, wallet and letter. He advanced to the front door, closed it behind him and vigilantly locked it.

Within a minute, Oliver entered the available elevator. Two eccentric strangers ogled his suit with particular interest. Oliver wondered why they sized him up, but decided to suppress his curiosity.

DING!

Oliver started rubbing his hands together with excitement. He couldn't wait to see Dr. Bell's face when she saw his new suit.

He proceeded to room 500 and rhythmically knocked with bony knuckles grazing over the wooden door.

Suddenly, he heard some shuffling and sliding of the lock from the top. She peered through the peephole and swung open the door.

"Oliver! Is that you, my dear? You look so handsome!" Dr. Bell exclaimed. Her head slightly tilted with endearment.

Oliver began to blush a little and shifted his shiny feet. "Thank you, Dr. Bell. I just wanted to say hi before heading out to the speech competition. I gotta go say hi to Deputy Jerry as well."

At once, Dr. Bell's face drained of all colour. She compulsively wrapped her arms around herself and strained to avoid Oliver's gaze.

"Dr. Bell?"

She still avoided Oliver's gaze, but turned her head in his direction. "My poor boy. Didn't you hear?"

Oliver started to feel apprehensive. Something about her tone made him uncomfortable. "Hear about what?" he squeaked.

Dr. Bell opened her mouth, but didn't say anything. She chewed her lip as she debated to say it. He stared intently at her, bracing himself for the announcement.

Finally, she looked at Oliver with glossy eyes. "Deputy Jerry is in the hospital."

22

The words stung like a venom-filled hornet. Oliver's legs almost buckled and it took all his effort to stand upright. His mouth dried up like a drought, unable to fathom the news. After a few attempts, Oliver asked, "What do you mean, in the hospital?"

Dr. Bell's dreary tone persisted. "He got into a fight with a jerk on the third floor, who refused to obey Deputy Jerry's orders about excessive noise. As a result, he broke his ribs and got a concussion."

Oliver stared in shock the whole time.

"He's been in the downtown hospital for about a week now. Doctors are hoping that things will improve, but he's unable to speak right now."

Instant flashbacks of being at the Honey Garden rushed through Oliver's brain. He was consumed with remorse.

"I'm sorry, Oliver. I know you have your big day and I don't mean to be a downer." Dr. Bell sympathized.

Oliver's phone buzzed. He stayed frozen and ignored it. The buzz sound grew louder.

"Aren't you going to check that?" Dr. Bell inquired.

Oliver meekly reached into his hip pocket, and with droopy eyes read the text message.

-Waiting for you outside.

Oliver dryly texted his response at a snail's pace.

-1 min.

"You should be on your way now. It's almost time for the Write Speech competition to begin." Dr. Bell motioned for him to leave.

Oliver refused to budge and firmly planted his polished shoes into the ground.

"I can't. I need to go see Deputy Jerry."

"But Oli-"

"I need to see him." Oliver was heavily panting. "Can you take me?"

"I'm not dressed to go out. Don't worry, I'll go see Deputy Jerry and keep him company."

He forcefully clenched his fists and without saying a word, hastened towards the elevator shaft. Dr. Bell gave a little wave and quickly closed her door.

Oliver furiously pressed the call down button. After a few seconds, he pressed it again and again. Agonized with the waiting time, Oliver bolted to the hallway stairwell. He panted in short breaths as his new shoes clattered down five floors.

I'm coming, Deputy Jerry. Just hang on.

He reached the bottom floor and paused, slightly bent over with resting hands on his knees. He noticed through the vestibule glass that a standard, blue compact car with "Write Speech" plastered on its side parked at the main entrance.

Oliver sprinted past the doors, darted towards the car and leaned his head through the rolled passenger window.

"Are you Oliver Masque?" the driver asked. He was a burly man, with a faded, cyan blue backwards cap and forest green t-shirt. He had both hands clutching the steering wheel.

"Yes." Oliver panted. "Look, an emergency came up and I desperately need to go to the downtown hospital along the way. Can you drop me off there?"

The driver scoffed and shook his head. "I'm only scheduled to drop you off at the Write Speech competition. What do I look like, a cab?"

The sass in the driver's voice riled Oliver up. "I know, but this is an em-er-gen-cy. A friend of mine is in critical danger."

The driver narrowed his dagger eyes to slits. "You're really testing my patience, boy. Are you getting in or not?"

"I need to go to the hospital," Oliver insisted.

The driver coldly glared straight through the windshield with feline eyes. "Good luck with that."

He rolled up the passenger window to Oliver's dismayed face. The driver put the car in "D" and roared off. Bits of dust and debris trailed behind the car as Oliver stared with disbelief.

He kicked the gravel furiously with his newly shined leather shoes. It faintly scratched up the sides, but he didn't care.

Oliver held a wider stance, clenched his fists and bitterly placed them on his waist. *Now what? I don't have a ride to go to the competition or to see Deputy Jerry.*

His heart raced faster and his breath was shallower. He periodically rubbed his right hand over his hair. The thought of seeing Deputy Jerry laying there in a hospital bed all by himself, in a pitiful state, grieved Oliver.

"Oliver!"

He turned around and squinted to figure out the source of the call.

Dr. Bell emerged out of the entryway and urgently waved in Oliver's direction. She wore a long, lavender skirt with matching lilac shirt and a pearl necklace.

"What happened?" Dr. Bell asked.

"My ride showed up and I wanted him to drop me off at the hospital since it was on the way, but the driver wouldn't let me." Oliver kicked the gravel and hanged his head low.

It hurt Dr. Bell to see Oliver's futile efforts for Deputy Jerry. "Come with me, we'll take my car."

Oliver lifted his head up. "Really?"

Dr. Bell glanced at her pearl watch. "Let's try to make this work. Hopefully, we can catch both Deputy Jerry and the competition."

Oliver immediately started walking to the right. "This way?"

"My car is on the other side." Dr. Bell pointed in the opposite direction.

Oliver sheepishly giggled at his mistake and jogged slightly to catch up with Dr. Bell. Her lavender skirt swished as she led the way to the outdoor parking lot.

She plucked out her car keys from her white laced purse. The minivan keys jingled as she directly pressed the unlock door button.

It made a loud chirping noise and Oliver hopped into the passenger's side. As Dr. Bell positioned herself in the driver's seat, Oliver slid his door closed and strapped on his seat belt. The dark leather upholstery was softer than any sofa he sat on.

Dr. Bell secured her seatbelt and assertively turned the ignition switch to the "on" position. The engine revved to life as she adjusted the A/C system.

Oliver glanced at the dashboard clock. 4:00 p.m.

He powered on the radio and tuned in to the 99.9 station.

"It's the most anticipated event of the year. People are already filling up seats. We'll be here covering this event and will have the latest scoop."

23

Wind fluttered through Oliver's hair as thick trees, vivid traffic signs and casual pedestrians whipped past.

Random advertisements were playing on the radio, but Oliver barely paid attention to them. Disturbing thoughts zoomed through his mind as he constantly squirmed in his seat.

"What's the matter?" Dr. Bell said, fixated on the road.

"Nothing." Oliver rested his elbow on the window sill.

Dr. Bell lowered the radio volume. "Oliver, I know how badly you want to see him. Just remember that he's under care with the nurses and doctors at the hospital."

Oliver glimpsed at the dashboard clock. 4:30 p.m., half-hour past the first round of registration.

She caught Oliver's worried glance. "Don't worry, people get held up all the time. They probably won't start the event until later on."

Oliver wanted to believe that, but he still felt apprehensive about being late.

"I'm curious to know why you decided to take part in this competition in the first place. Do you like public speaking?"

Oliver solemnly gazed at the rear view mirror. "Deputy Jerry was the one who encouraged me to do it. He saw something in me that others didn't."

"I'm sure he'll have a-"

Suddenly, Oliver geared up the volume on the radio. "I think I heard they're about to start."

The booming radio voice pierced through the minivan.

"Welcome, everybody! Allow me to formally begin this year's Write Speech competition! My name is Chip Turner and I'll be your emcee today. The Write Speech competition has been around for many, many years. It strongly values superb communication abilities because, let's face it, not all of us speak well. From family misunderstandings, down to the simple order at your favourite fast food restaurant. At Write Speech, it's all about delivering clear messages, and for this year's theme, we're talking about Helping Humanity Holistically."

Oliver sat motionless, absorbing every word. Dr. Bell stayed silent as she carefully drove.

"Yes, this is a broad theme. But, in doing so, we're giving our ten contestants the freedom to address this much needed topic from any angle they desire. We hope you'll gather some insight for your own lives. Now, let's begin with the first contestant, shall we? Please welcome, Veronica McCoy!"

Oliver quickly glanced at Dr. Bell. "How much farther do we have to go?"

Dr. Bell rolled to a stop at a red light. "It's about thirty minutes away. Remember, we're going downtown and traffic is a nightmare."

Oliver despairingly tilted his head back and closed his eyes in defeat. No matter how much he wanted things to go faster, he couldn't control the traffic. Suddenly, he felt drained.

Dr. Bell sensed that Oliver required rest, so she abruptly shut off the radio. Oliver motioned with his hand to switch it back on. "Please, just lower the volume."

Dr. Bell dutifully lowered the volume. Oliver was half-aware, but caught snippets of the speeches in progress.

"Humanity calls for more selflessness, not selfishness. More 'we,' not 'me.' Isn't it amazing that we can spend years living beside our neighbours, yet not know their names or their occupations?"

"The only way we can help humanity holistically is to think of ourselves as pieces of a puzzle. It's not just made up of one piece. We each have to make our contributions to complete the picture."

"The cure for humanity is proper education and sincerity. You can grow up with the wrong information your whole life, but if you are sincere, you will find what you are looking for."

Oliver desperately tried to concentrate on the speeches, but wearily dozed off as he leaned back on the headrest. Oliver's throat vibrated as he lightly snored. Dr. Bell compassionately switched off the radio and drove in serenity.

***

"Wake up, sleepy head. We're here."

Oliver gasped awake. 5:30 p.m.

Dr. Bell grinned. "The annoying announcer said they finished the first wave of five contenders and now there's a break until the next batch go up."

Oliver quickly unfastened his seat belt and actively leaped out of the minivan. He slammed the passenger door and glanced up at the luminous Downtown Hospital sign in front of the sleek, rectangular building.

Oliver gulped as he saw a group of paramedics working together to take a child out on a stretcher from an ambulance. She screeched in pain as she appeared to clutch her dislocated knee.

Oliver made haste to the main entrance while Dr. Bell locked the car door. He jolted past the sliding door and was taken aback by the blinding, white colour. The main reception, general ward and seating lounges were all chalk white.

Oliver ran up to the curved reception desk. A headset lady with a milky white uniform sat on the other side. "Hi, how may I help you?"

"I need to see Deputy Jerry. What room is he in?" Oliver struggled for breath.

"I'm sorry. For privacy reasons, we can't disclose our patients," the receptionist said.

Oliver huffed and grew impatient. As soon as he was about to lash out, Dr. Bell appeared and stood by his side. She noticed his uptight demeanor. "Oliver, how about you go sit on one of those sofas and I'll take care of this?"

Shoulders heaving, Oliver went and sat down. He wasn't able to decipher Dr. Bell's words, but examined her frantic gestures and witnessed the receptionist making phone calls.

After what seemed to be an eternity, Dr. Bell nodded towards the receptionist, hastened towards Oliver and motioned for him to get up. "He's in room C355 upstairs."

Oliver jumped up. "Wha-How did you do it?"

Dr. Bell smiled sweetly. "I just explained the situation and the receptionist was sympathetic. Let's go."

They advanced to the giant map located beside the reception desk. The map featured a 3D rendering of the hospital interior, complete with all the room labels.

"Right here, third floor." Dr. Bell pointed to the orange block with C355 text.

"And the elevators are straight ahead." Oliver noted the grey square symbol with an "X" in the middle.

They walked briskly to the milky white elevators and got on. Once they arrived on the third floor, Dr. Bell lurched forward. "It's this way. I remember from the map."

With every step, Oliver grew increasingly anxious. They wearily moved down the corridor and passed by various patients. Individuals in wheelchairs or with wooden crutches carried the same cold, lifeless expression on their faces. Oliver's hair follicles on his neck contracted in fear.

C355 loomed into view and they entered through the door. A petite nurse with an aqua green apron and hygiene cap blocked their path. "What are you here for?"

Oliver blurted out, "To see Deputy Jerry."

The nurse's eyelashes fluttered like feathers. "Okay, you two must be the people reception called."

Oliver and Dr. Bell solemnly followed the nurse. There were dark purple, cottony curtains for the individual patients. They were arranged like cubicles in an office. The nonstop beep of monitors saturated the room.

She led them to a cubicle in the far corner of the room. With a swift motion, the nurse slid open the curtain. Oliver nearly crumbled at the sight and Dr. Bell covered her mouth in sadness.

24

Deputy Jerry was sprawled out on his hospital bed, with numerous tubes hooked up to his arms. A sonogram constantly bleeped as clear liquid slowly filled up a tube, drip by drip. His veiny head was propped up with numerous pillows and his frail appearance aged him over 30 years.

Oliver inhaled deeply and stepped forward. The nurse extended her arm to obstruct his path. "He is in critical condition. His ribs are broken and he suffered a concussion. He is aware of what's around him, but he can't respond. Don't try to force him to talk, as he needs all the energy he can get for recovery."

Oliver stared at Deputy Jerry, the once vibrant, active, healthy steed of Altitude Apartments. Now, dwindled into a fragile being that looked like he could be swept away by a breeze.

Oliver turned to Dr. Bell. "What should we do?"

Dr. Bell shook her head. "We should probably leave. Give him some space." She turned and walked to the door.

"We can't just leave him here!" Oliver yelled.

The nurse shushed but he disregarded her. "We have to stay and be here for him," Oliver said firmly.

Hopelessness flickered in Dr. Bell's eyes. "What can we do? The nurse says he needs to be alone to recover."

Oliver bent down and his knees collided with the floor. "The last thing he needs is to be alone. He needs a friend to be there for him," Oliver choked.

The nurse tapped on Oliver's back. "Sir, if you are going to continue to act wildly, I'm going to have to escort you out."

Oliver remained on all fours. A tear streamed down his face and dripped to the ground. "How can I go talk about saving humanity when I can't even save one friend?"

Dr. Bell pursed her lips together and fought back tears of her own. She witnessed the unbearable distress in Oliver and tried to brainstorm a plan. Suddenly, she noticed some fidgeting at the hospital bed. "Oliver, look! Deputy Jerry is moving!"

Oliver immediately turned around and sniffled. Deputy Jerry intricately waved his right hand. His feeble fingers swayed towards the door as the tubes connected to his arm faintly rattled.

Oliver was perplexed. "What are you trying to say, Deputy Jerry?"

"I think he's saying you should go." Dr. Bell said.

Oliver slowly stood up. "I can't leave him here by himself. He needs someone."

The nurse tried to persuade Oliver. "Sir, your friend is in good hands."

"No, he's right."

Oliver and the nurse swiveled to face Dr. Bell.

"Deputy Jerry needs a familiar face to stand by him. I'm sorry for not seeing this sooner, Oliver. I will be with him while you go share your message to the world." Dr. Bell said.

Oliver's face lit up as he rubbed his nose. "But how am I supposed to get there?"

Dr. Bell reached into her sewn pockets and pulled out three $20 bills. "Here, take a taxi. This should cover the fare. Hurry,

Oliver! They might be starting the second batch of contestants soon."

Oliver graciously took the money and slid it in his back pocket. "Thank you."

He soothingly looked at Deputy Jerry with steeply arched brows. "I promise to make you proud."

Oliver bolted to the door, paused and earnestly glanced back. Dr. Bell waved and mouthed the word "go." A tender smile graced his lips as he left.

Dr. Bell turned to the nurse. "Thank you for all your help and patience. Can we change the TV channel to see the Write Speech competition?" She motioned to the wall mounted television near Deputy Jerry's bed.

The nurse nodded. "Certainly. Let me get the remote." She trotted away.

Dr. Bell glanced at Deputy Jerry and let a soft sigh. *You can do it, Oliver.*

***

"What's the phone number for a taxi?"

"We have a special phone line for taxis right over here." The receptionist pointed towards the bronze landline on the far left.

"Or you could try seeing if taxis are outside. Sometimes, they randomly stop by since we're in the downtown area."

Oliver thanked her and slid his way across the counter. He grasped the antique-looking phone handle, but felt a surge of impulsiveness kicking in.

Maybe there's a taxi hanging around.

He slammed down the phone, dashed out the hospital exit doors and placed his hand on his crinkled forehead as he scanned the area for any lone taxi in the drop off area.

He resembled a lost sailor at sea. *Come on.*

Much to Oliver's delight, a bumble bee taxi van pulled up. He waited until the taxi driver unloaded his client's belongings from the trunk, exchanged goodbyes and scurried back to the driver's seat.

"Oh!" the taxi driver was startled at Oliver's determined head poking through the passenger window.

"Can you take me to the Downtown Convention Centre? I'm in a *really* big hurry." Oliver pleaded.

The taxi driver was stunned at the sudden request. Oliver's puppy eyes glimmered.

"Hop on, but don't scare me again," the taxi driver warned.

25

Oliver launched into the passenger seat and eagerly buckled up. The taxi driver's bushy brows beetled with astonishment.

"You look like a jittery rabbit." The taxi driver inputted information on his fare machine, adjusted the rear-view mirror and accelerated out of the hospital drop-off area.

Oliver deftly glanced at the digital clock on the taxi dashboard. 6:00 p.m.

"So, mind telling me what the fuss is all about?" the taxi driver scratched his neck acne scar. His slicked back, platinum blond hair accentuated his prominent nose.

"I have to be delivering a speech and I'm ridiculously late." Oliver nervously gazed out of his window.

The taxi driver nodded. "Yep, I get those kinds of customers a lot. Fancy public speakers like yourself, giving important talks. Me, I don't like talking to large crowds."

The rubber tires slowly rotated as the cab moved forward. Perpetual honking filled the air and inaudible shouts blazed through the atmosphere.

"Yep, I'm a simple guy. Just like talking one-on-one. Makes it easier to connect, you know what I mean?" the taxi driver sucked his teeth.

Oliver's facial expression turned sour. *What's wrong with this guy?*

"Anyways, what are you talking about?" the taxi driver cast an eye at Oliver.

"It's a message for humanity."

"Woohoo! 'Message for humanity.' We've got a lot of problems and I don't think a speech can help fix that," the taxi driver laughed.

"How much longer until we get to the Downtown Convention Centre?" Oliver cut him off.

The taxi driver cracked his neck. "Looks like 15 minutes or so. You're lucky this place is nearby, but unlucky with all this traffic."

A silver car swayed and attempted to overtake them off. The taxi driver smashed his foot on the brake and irritatingly honked his horn.

"Gotta deal with these brainless buffoons on a daily basis," the taxi driver spat.

Maybe if I rest, all of this will go away.

"What's the matter with you, boy? Tired already? Don't you have some message to humanity to deliver?" the taxi driver snickered.

Oliver's eyelids flew open like a sudden door opening. He turned on the radio to the 99.9 station.

`"Now for the 6th competitor, Rick Chaser-"`

Oliver keenly blasted the radio volume.

"Hey, what do you think you're doing?" the taxi driver barked.

"Shhhh! It's the speaking competition," Oliver pointed excitedly to the radio.

"I don't care what it is. You don't ever touch my radio." The taxi driver switched it to pop music and bobbed his head in sync with the tunes.

Oliver huffed and turned it back to 99.9. The taxi driver

snarled and turned it back.

"Come on! I need to hear what's going on at the competition!" Oliver exclaimed.

"You're in MY taxi now," the taxi driver said menacingly.

Oliver gave up. "Fine, just turn it off!" He crossed his arms and stared out the window.

Last thing he needed was an angry customer. The taxi driver growled and switched off the radio. "What's the big deal with this public speaking thing, anyway?"

"You wouldn't understand," Oliver mumbled.

They drove for a few minutes in silence. Advertisements promoting various products competed for attention in the downtown core. Chaotic traffic was congested, and Oliver occasionally fidgeted around in his seat.

"Try me," the taxi driver said, without taking his eyes off the road.

"What?"

"You said earlier that I wouldn't understand why you're doing this whole public speaking thing. Try me," the taxi driver insisted.

Oliver wasn't sure if this was a mockery. "I don't know."

"Well, isn't that something? Here you are, on your way to deliver some big speech for humanity and you don't even know why you're doing it. Pathetic, just like I thought."

Oliver's jaw clenched and bared his teeth. His nostrils flared as his words spewed out like a volcano eruption.

"What do you know about public speaking? All you do is sit in your seat and drive everyone around. Maybe one day you'll get a real job!"

Suddenly, Oliver jolted forward. The seat buckle gripped tightly on his stomach as Oliver's head nearly hit the dashboard. The taxi driver kept his foot on the break and stared coldly at Oliver.

"Get out."

Oliver's mouth gaped open in shock. "I-I'm sorry, sir."

"Get. Out."

Within seconds, a long line of vehicles formed behind them. Blaring honks accompanied with profanity frightened Oliver.

"Sir, please forgive me. I-I didn't mean that. Please..."

HOOOOONK.

Oliver felt his pulse beating in his ears. His hands started to tremble in an odd rhythm while his stomach churned. Oliver wanted to curl up, away from everything.

"You better be careful of what you say, boy. You say the wrong thing to the wrong person and you'll be sorry."

The taxi driver put his foot on the gas pedal and continued onwards. Oliver sat up and didn't say anything.

Soon, an elegant Downtown Convention Centre sign loomed into view. The hustle and bustle of downtown city life illuminated the streets. The taxi driver put on his right turn indicator signal and swerved into the single lane drop off area.

A lady with sunglasses and a bright orange vest stood at the curb and motioned for the taxi driver to lower his window. "You need to quickly move out for traffic flow."

The taxi driver pressed the button on his cab fare and said, "That'll be $50."

Oliver unbuckled his seatbelt and reached into his pocket for the wad of cash. "Here's $60. Keep the change." He swiftly unlocked the door and stepped out.

The taxi driver roared off as Oliver stood in front of the Downtown Convention Centre.

26

Oliver was temporarily mesmerized by the sheer grandeur of the place. Tall, sophisticated columns wedged between the lavish doors. The fluorescent lights beaming from the pillars radiantly shimmered against the gradual darkening of the evening.

Oliver joined a wave of people entering inside and was greeted by the doorman. He wore a high brimmed hat, sharp Stewards jacket with a gold trim and formal white gloves. The doorman smiled at Oliver as he graciously stepped aside and opened the door.

Wow!

Fancy water fountains gushed wondrously across the main hall. Giant chandeliers with stylish light fixtures prominently hanged. The glossy floor composed of bold black marble tiles featuring unique patterns.

Oliver was momentarily spellbound, absorbing the stunning atmosphere. He dazedly walked, turning his head from side to side, admiring all the wonderful designs.

"Oops, sorry!" Oliver clumsily bumped into a lady with a beret, who simply shrugged it off.

Oliver blushed slightly and noticed a wall mounted, gigantic, rustic clock with roman numerals in the middle of the reception area. 7:15 p.m.

Oliver snapped out of his dream state. *Where is the Write Speech competition?*

Hundreds of people assembled throughout the labyrinth halls and each room looked similar to the one before.

"Excuse me, do you know where the Write Speech competition is? Excuse me?"

Oliver tried asking random strangers but to no avail. Either they truly didn't know or they didn't want to help.

After a few moments of unsuccessful attempts, Oliver finally stumbled across a wooden sign hanging from the ceiling with an arrow pointing downwards. After pushing through congested crowds, he realized the arrow led to the main reception area.

Oliver dashed past the line to a receptionist with a white and blue Write Speech nametag. "Hi, where is the Write Speech competition?"

The receptionist glared at him. "Sir, please go back to the line."

Oliver's heart skipped a beat. "I'm one of the finalists. Something tragic came up and I had rush my way over here. Can you please show me where I can go?"

The receptionist glanced at her watch. "It doesn't matter since it's about to end soon."

"Look, my name is Oliver Masque. You'll find me in the system!" Oliver pointed to the receptionist's computer.

She reluctantly sighed and speedily typed his name on the computer. Oliver heard her long fingernails clashing against the keyboard.

"Just give me a few seconds," the receptionist said.

"Take your time," Oliver said wearily.

He apprehensively gawked at the marvelous decor, with hopes of distracting himself and maintaining composure. He was fixed on the enormous, elaborate mirror behind the reception desk but caught a glimpse of his worried expression.

He noticed a flower arrangement near him and stared at it. There were yellow, red and purple flowers in a circular design.

"Sir?"

Oliver bounced back to meet the receptionist's attention. "Yes?"

"I'm sorry, but registration was promptly at 4:00 p.m., and since we're almost wrapping up the event, we can't allow any more participants," the receptionist said.

The words hit Oliver like a ton of bricks. "B-b-but..."

"I'm sorry," the receptionist said firmly.

Oliver studied her with piercing scrutiny, gently tapped his hand on the desk and let out a breath of defeat.

"Could you at least tell me what room it's in?"

"Room D. It's down the hall and onto your left," the receptionist pointed.

"Thanks." Oliver steadily trudged away from the desk and glanced upwards at the giant clock. 7:40 p.m.

What now?

Oliver sagged his shoulders and strode through the congregated areas. It dawned on him that there was a large, chestnut wooden sign hanging from the top with almost invisible strings. It read "Rooms A-G on left."

A sea of well-dressed people chattering filled the scene as Oliver passed through the various rooms. A...B...C...D.

He arrived at "D." It was the largest conference room on the left side. There were massive columns on either side of the maroon door. Long, velvet red stanchions were lined up on either end.

There was a young man sitting at a table on the side. He appeared to be the gatekeeper, controlling traffic in and out. Oliver was about to barge through the doors until he noticed the gatekeeper viewed him with suspicion.

Oliver reeled up to him. "Excuse me, is this the Write Speech competition?"

"Yes, do you have your ticket?"

"Oh, actually, I'm a speaker."

"We're about to finish," the gatekeeper said flatly.

Oliver was getting tired of hearing that. "I *know*."

He suddenly dropped the aggravated tone once he saw the gatekeeper's eyes narrow. "I mean, I know, but there's got to be some way to get in. You see, my friend was in the hospital and you know it was just unfortunate, but I had to decide to see him or not, but you know-"

"Okay, whatever dude. I've been working here all day and tired of this nonsense. I don't know if they'll still allow you to go at this late time, but you can go through the backstage."

Oliver wanted to leap for joy, but contained it. He cleared his throat and tried to sound professional. "Thank you. How do I get there?"

The gatekeeper waved his hand. "I can't leave this table, but there should be some volunteers floating around. Wait, I see one. Yo, Cindy!"

Oliver glanced at the direction that the gatekeeper called out. A girl with auburn hair strolled her way through and excitedly stood beside Oliver. "What's up?" she beamed.

"Could you take this guy to see Chip backstage? He says

he's a speaker, but I don't know if they'll allow him to get on stage at this time," the gatekeeper said.

"Sure, follow me," Cindy chirped.

27

Oliver felt like he was about to enter a lavish, prestigious palace. The intricate, handcrafted design on the door hypnotized him.

Cindy placed her hand on the shiny, gold handle. The handle was long and emitted an aura of royalty.

Oliver was giddy and bouncing all around on the inside. *This is it.*

Cindy turned the handle and it made a loud click. It was the sweetest sound Oliver ever heard.

Oliver's heart pounded hysterically as Cindy swung the door open. For a moment, he froze in place, overwhelmed by the sheer brilliance of the room.

Cindy waved at him. "It's alright, you can enter."

The place was packed with 5000 people sitting tightly in their soft, velvet seats. They were arranged in clusters, so the arrangement appeared grid-like from the ceiling.

Cindy continued to lead the way, occasionally glancing back to check if Oliver was within close reach. He glanced from side to side, mesmerized by the awe-inspiring sight.

A speaker was delivering her speech for the competition. "You can't expect people to lend a helping hand if you don't offer yours. You get what you give. It's that simple."

Oliver was enraptured by the scene as he navigated through the centre aisle. Regular attendees eyed him, annoyed by the disturbance while some glued their gaze to the speaker.

They were near the main stage, where Oliver almost fainted from the amazing sight. The stage featured a curved top with red curtains and superior microphone stand.

Oliver slowed down and admired the beauty of the dynamic microphone. It's wire coil and crisp audio quality almost made him drool.

A group of volunteers with their respective name tags hung around the main stage. Cindy and Oliver moved past them and proceeded towards a door marked "Private."

"Excuse me, you aren't allowed back here," a volunteer tapped Oliver's arm.

Cindy quickly jumped in. "It's okay, he's with me. He's going to see Chip."

The volunteer relaxed and let them go inside. Oliver was about to go pale from the constant barrage of checkpoints.

It was like a fashion dressing room. The word "Chip" was on top of a stylish mirror with many light bulbs on the sides. A man sitting in a swivel chair discretely brushed his coarse, brown hair into a comb over style.

Cindy walked up to the man and lightly tapped on his shoulder. "Chip, there's someone here to see you."

Suddenly, the man stopped brushing and stood up. His dominating 6'6 figure towered over Oliver. His smart tuxedo with a platinum striped bowtie, black satin vest and beige flower exuded power.

"What can I do for you?"

Oliver recognized that voice from the radio. *This is Chip Turner, the emcee for the Write Speech competition!* "We-well, you see, I'm supposed to be a speaker today."

Chip twisted his face into a disdained grimace."We're almost done. What's your name?"

"Oliver Masque."

Chip lightly grazed his chin. "That name sounds familiar. I think the organizers mentioned an 'Oliver' for the finals."

Oliver nodded his head excitedly. "Yes, exactly! But, there was an emergency with a friend at a hospital and that's why I'm late."

Chip irritatedly referred to his diamond watch. "I'm supposed to be up there in two minutes and start the voting process. I don't know how you can give your speech at this time."

"Please, give me a chance," Oliver begged.

"Hey, Chip. It looks like this guy had a rough day with his friend in the hospital. Why not make him give a shorter speech?" Cindy shrugged.

Chip focused his gaze on Cindy then to Oliver's eyes. His piercing gaze made Oliver uncomfortable, but he summoned the strength to stare down Chip.

Chip stayed silent for a few seconds then held out five fingers in front of Oliver's face. "You have five minutes. I'll stall for a bit more time."

"Thank you," Oliver whispered.

Cindy smiled. "Great!"

"Okay, now please leave. I have to go back and emcee."

Cindy and Oliver obediently withdrew from Chip's dressing room and shuffled to the side of the stage. Oliver's heart was pounding like a racehorse. He wasn't sure how to condense his original ten minute speech into five minutes.

Cindy looked at Oliver and raised two thumbs up. "Good luck!" She pranced back through the aisle, leaving Oliver alone beside the fancy stairs up to the stage.

Suddenly, Chip emerged from his dressing room and stood beside Oliver. He could smell Chip's zesty, musk cologne scent. The speaker on stage wrapped up her final thoughts.

"In conclusion, let's all work together for a brighter future. If you want to grow a tree, you must plant the seed today. Thank you."

The audience roared with applause. Chip climbed the stairs and acquired the microphone as she descended down the stairs to the left.

"Awe-inspiring speech, Wendy. Indeed, we reap what we sow. Now, I know I mentioned earlier that we were going to start voting, but someone rather unexpected showed up. His name is Oliver Masque and he will be presenting a condensed version of his speech to humanity. With that, please welcome Oliver Masque!"

A polite applause ensued. Just like that, Oliver was in the spotlight. He nearly stumbled on the steps, but somehow managed to make his way to the centre of the stage. He nervously shook Chip's hand, grabbed the microphone and stared out into the audience.

28

"H-hi everyone. S-sorry, I'm late; a friend of mine was in the hospital so..."

Oliver stopped midsentence when he saw a familiar face in the crowd. Mrs. Wilkins sat near the front, and waved excitedly to Oliver. A few of his classmates were also seated beside her.

Oliver cleared his throat and then the microphone squeaked. People immediately plugged their fingers into their ears with loud groans of discomfort.

Oliver directed the microphone away from his face and the sound subsided. "Sorry about that. Technical problems, hehe..."

Oliver wanted to bolt out of the stage and run home, away from all the angry faces. But, he forced himself to stay. He closed his eyes, took a deep breath and began.

"My name is Oliver Masque and I hate people. I hate it when people don't acknowledge my existence. I hate it when people don't give me a chance to show what I'm good at. I hate it when people judge me at first glance. I know this is a conference for helping humanity, but hear me out."

There was an air of uneasiness in the crowd. Perplexed audience members glanced at each other and asked what was going on. Chip stood at the bottom of the stairs nervously picking at his goatee.

"Maybe I should explain where these feelings come from. You see, my parents split up when I was five. I don't really remember them, but all I do know is that neither of them wanted to raise me as a single parent. Instead, they agreed to put me in a foster home and that's how I grew up. Foster home after foster home."

Oliver sauntered across the stage.

"Even at that young age, I was always wondering why my mom and dad didn't come to pick me up. Why was I suddenly with a bunch of random strangers? When they first took me into a foster home, I cried out for my mom. They kept telling me that she wasn't going to be around anymore."

Mrs. Wilkins dabbed a tear away from her eye.

"My dad did not want to do anything with me. Loneliness began to consume me. Every day, I would see parents hugging their loved ones and I didn't have anyone to go to. I always asked myself why they never wanted me."

Oliver started to choke back a few tears, but cleared his throat a number of times.

"The only thing I have of them is this letter."

Oliver steadily took out the envelope from his right blazer pocket. The paper crinkled as he carefully opened the letter, while holding the microphone in the other hand.

"Apparently, the people at the foster home told me my dad was a great poet and left me this letter when I was dropped off. I don't know if that's true or not, but at least I like to think so."

Oliver, my only son

Love yourself and the world

In spite of things undone

Visionaries are unfurled

Every person that you lift

Remember that is your gift

"Every time I look at this poem, I feel like such a failure. If the two people who are supposed to love me unconditionally rejected me, then how can anyone else be with me?"

Oliver folded up the letter and placed it back in his pocket.

"So, I personally made a vow to myself to avoid people. I didn't want to do anything with anyone. I even purposely screamed my throat raw every night to make it harder to talk to people."

Oliver moved back to the centre of the stage.

"But when someone decided to stand up for me, I began to think someone actually cared about me. When I was constantly made fun of on Two Cents, an anonymous person defended me. I can't even thank him or her properly, but I just want to let you know that if you are listening, thank you."

Oliver solemnly held his hand to his heart and bowed slightly with appreciation.

"That's not all. Deputy Jerry saw something in me that I didn't see in myself. He taught me that I could be way more than I was."

Oliver cast his eyes down at the ground.

"Now, he's in the hospital, fighting for his life. I feel like I've failed him. A man who spent his whole life trying to protect others needed someone to protect him. I had the desire to stay, but luckily Dr. Bell is by his side. She is an amazing person, always willing to help."

Oliver glanced down at Chip, who made a twirling motion with his fingers to signal wrap up.

"Since I'm running short on time, the one thing I will leave you with is to make every person you meet feel worthwhile. I can't tell you how painful it is to feel that you're worthless in this world. If it weren't for those people who took time out of their day to make me feel like a human being, then I probably wouldn't be here today. So, thank you."

Oliver dropped the microphone from his face and waited to hand it over. Chip trotted up to the centre of the stage, took the microphone from Oliver's hands and raised it up to his mouth.

"Well, that was quite a different speech than the ones we've heard previously. You can make your way down and mingle with the other speakers, Oliver." Chip gestured to the left.

Oliver immediately rambled off the stage and gradually went down the stairs.

Chip turned back to the stunned audience. "Alright, everyone that's all the speeches for this year's Write Speech competition. At this time, please take out your devices and go on the link projected on the screen to cast your vote for this year's winner."

29

W as it something I said?

Oliver glanced down at his red suit, inspecting any dirt or something physically unappealing. Nothing.

Oliver staggered to the speaker's lounge area and was faced with eight pairs of eyes icily staring at him. The harsh gazes started to weigh him down as he strove towards the refreshment stand. After a few steps, the room burst with excitement.

"What a heartfelt speech!"

"What was your name again?"

"It was so sad and inspiring at the same time."

Floods of questions and comments were aimed at Oliver. He tried responding to each query but found it difficult to keep up with the overlapping conversations.

"It was no big deal. I just spoke what came from here," Oliver pointed to his chest.

"But it must have been so difficult for you to talk about your parents like that," Veronica said.

Oliver shrugged. "You can't cry forever."

"Where on earth did you get that red suit? It matches perfectly with the curtains in the background," another speaker asked.

Oliver grinned. "Taylored Suits is your answer."

More questions and comments were directed at Oliver. It was so exhilarating for him to be acknowledged by so many people at once. Oliver was smiling from ear to ear. However, in the midst of the crowd, Oliver noticed someone lurking in the background.

Rick leaned against the wall, arms and legs crossed while staring at the group huddle. He donned a navy blue blazer, creamy white tie and salmon dress shoes.

What is he going to do?

Oliver was worried Rick would try to tarnish his experience after receiving such wonderful compliments. Instantly, Oliver recalled the harsh words over Two Cents and the painstaking hand squeezes.

Maybe he's just waiting for the right moment to make fun of me in front of everyone. Something like, 'Did you all know he called his teacher Mommy?'

Oliver instinctively rubbed his hands together and tried to ignore Rick. Maybe if he didn't make a big fuss, Rick would leave him alone. After a few more minutes of Oliver conversing with the fellow finalists, he began to relax. Rick remained quiet the entire time.

After what seemed to be a blissful eternity, a Write Speech volunteer entered the room. She waved her arms to garner attention. "You can all come back outside right now. The results are in."

Everyone stopped chatting and shuffled back to the stage in a single-file formation. The volunteer stiffly held the door open for all of them. Oliver was sandwiched at the middle of the line while Rick was the last person out.

"All the finalists, please join me up here on stage," Chip instructed.

The first thing Oliver noticed was the giant, shiny trophy cup beside Chip. It was about 3 feet tall, and created from pure gold. The trophy had two handles on either side and seemed weighty. It rested on a star studded table and the Write Speech logo featured prominently on the table banner.

Reverting back to their single-file formation, the finalists proceeded up the marble stairs and moved to the centre of the stage. Commercial photographers hung around the stage, snapping digital images with their expensive cameras.

"Let's have a huge round of applause for our finalists!" Chip exclaimed.

A thunderous applause filled the air. Oliver felt like a king. He was so honoured to be on stage and hearing the deafening cheer. Oliver made sure to smile for the constant snapshots.

He peeked to his left, the finalists were all stone faced. He peeked to his right, no signs of joy. Oliver eased his smile and attempted to chisel out a more serious expression.

"This year, we have an exceptional batch of competitors. As promised, they delivered outstanding speeches from a variety of different angles. Some talked about the environment, others talked about social patterns. Some even shared their own personal life experiences to really bring this topic to life." Chip said.

Oliver slightly curled up his lips.

"The winner of this year's Write Speech competition exemplifies true dignity, persuasion and unparalleled communication abilities. This individual has exemplified what it means to be a leader, connecting with people on a deeper level."

Oliver started to shift his feet in anticipation. His shiny shoes gleaned as he moved them from side to side.

"Opportunities like this only come once a year, and those who have done a fantastic job here at Write Speech will most assuredly have a phenomenal public speaking career ahead of them."

Oliver could hardly contain himself. *This is my time.* The constant barrage of snapshots continued.

"This year's champion truly understands the power of speech, and with the right words, persuaded the majority of this audience to vote for him. And so, it is my honour and duty to present this year's Write Speech winner to..."

30

"Rick Chaser!"

Immediately, the speakers in the lineup began clapping in unison along with the thunderous wave of 5000 enthusiastic audience members.

Rick's nose and forehead scrunched up with one eyebrow raised. The speakers beside him slapped their hands on his back, congratulating him.

Oliver felt his intestines tie up like a knot in his stomach. His mind temporarily froze as he struggled to register the winner's name.

He saw Mrs. Wilkins standing up and clapping enthusiastically. Oliver wanted to put his hands together, but it was too painful for him to bear.

I'm sorry, Deputy Jerry and Dr. Bell.

Oliver felt sharp pangs and tears were uncontrollably running down his face. He pushed himself away from the lineup and sprinted to the stairs. He was sniffling and rubbing his red sleeve over his face with every step he took.

He trotted down the aisle, passed the volunteers and ignored the ecstatic crowd. *No one cares if I leave.*

Now the tears were streaming faster. The people were focused on the main stage, unwavered at Oliver moving in the opposite direction.

Cameras kept flashing and people were constantly chanting, "Speech! Speech! Speech!"

On the stage, Chip waved for Rick to stand beside him. Rick approached him, took the microphone, and looked on to the charged crowd. People cheered at the top of their lungs, while fist pumping the air.

Rick motioned everyone to sit down. The room eventually dwindled down to an absence of noise. He sharply sucked air into his abdomen and spoke.

"I'm sorry, but I can't accept this."

Time stood still as people's mouths gaped wide open. Oliver's hands froze on the exit door.

"I am not your rightful winner of the Write Speech competition. He is." Rick pointed to Oliver and suddenly everyone couldn't pry their eyes off him.

"Oliver did something admirable today. He was vulnerable and shared something so incredibly personal. Yet, we just brushed it off. Believe me, I also understand your pain of loneliness."

Oliver deliberately dropped his hands and lowered his shoulders.

"I wanted to break you but you never retaliated against me. I always thought if I showed the class what a loser you were, then it would make me popular. As an only child starving for attention, I guess I'm the lowlife. Rick the Prick."

Oliver's jaw retracted and tightened his neck muscles. He rolled his eyes skyward to prevent the bottled up tears from escaping.

"If more people tried following your genuine nature, I think we would be one step closer to helping humanity holistically. Come on up, my friend," Rick waved.

Oliver furrowed his brow and quivered his lower lip. His lean legs cemented in place.

Rick spoke into the microphone. "I know you're hesitating because I wasn't the nicest to you. But, believe me Oliver, you are the true Write Speech champion."

Oliver's shock melted away. He continuously sniffled as he slowly trekked towards the stage.

5000 audience members leapt to their feet in a ripple effect and loudly applauded with his every step. "Ol-iv-er! Ol-iv-er! Ol-iv-er!"

Oliver cautiously climbed up the stage to Rick's smiling face. Rick promptly extended his hand to Oliver, mouthed the words "don't worry" and the two firmly shook hands.

Crystalline tears flowed down Mrs. Wilkins' cheeks as she merrily joined the collective chant.

***

He stabilized his ailing arms on the bed as the tube wires wiggled. The woolly blankets shuffled slightly as he moved. His shaky left bare foot landed on the ice-cool floor tiles. Wheezing, his rickety right bare foot brushed the chilly ground. Dr. Bell anchored herself as he leaned on her as a crutch.

His blotched hand clutched desperately at his heaving chest. Unstable heart beats lost its intrinsic rhythm.

The corners of his frozen lips fought to curl upwards, as he faintly witnessed Oliver hugging the Write Speech trophy on the screen.

Beep. Beep. Beeeeeeep.

Author's Message

Dear Reader,

I hope you had a memorable experience with this story.

After completing a creative writing course at the University of Toronto and becoming a Toastmasters Competent Communicator, I gravitated towards the treasure of storytelling.

It's like you can transport to a new world, filled with captivating characters and enthralling environments, by simply reading words on a page.

I'd say if we told more compelling stories, it would be easier to learn life's greatest lessons.

If you'd like to know more information, you are more than welcome to visit my website.

mohammedmaxwelhasan.com

Or you can feel free to contact me directly via email.
mohammedmaxwel@gmail.com

I'm excited to hear your thoughts about "Can't Escape" and always open to feedback. Looking forward to hear from you!

Sincerely,

Mohammed Maxwel Hasan

www.ingramcontent.com/pod-product-compliance
Lightning Source LLC
Chambersburg PA
CBHW020251150626
46552CB00020B/770